Also by Geoffrey Malone

Brunner
Torn Ear
Kimba
Crocodile River
Elephant Ben
Wolf!
Cadoc
Tiger!

Other titles available from Hodder Children's Books

Eager
Eager's Nephew
Eager and the Mermaid
Helen Fox

Airborn
Skybreaker
Sunwing
Silverwing
Firewing
Kenneth Oppel

PIRATES

GEOFFREY MALONE

Hodder
Children's
Books

A division of Hachette Children's Books

First published in Great Britain in 2008
by Hodder Children's Books

A Catalogue record for this book is available from the British Library

ISBN 978 0 340 89359 3

Typeset in AGaramond by Avon DataSet Ltd,
Bidford on Avon, Warwickshire

Printed and bound in Great Britain by
CPI Bookmarque, Croydon, CR0 4TD

The paper and board used in this paperback by Hodder Children's Books
are natural recyclable products made from wood grown in
sustainable forests. The manufacturing processes conform to the
environmental regulations of the country of origin.

Hodder Children's Books
a division of Hachette Children's Books
338 Euston Road, London NW1 3BH
An Hachette Livre UK Company

*Beverley Birch, whose editorial wisdom and
enthusiasm have helped me through many books.
In gratitude and friendship.*

PLANNED TRACK OF THE SEROTA STAR
UP THE MALACCA STRAIT:

TAIWAN

H CHINA SEA

PHILIPPINES

PHILIPPINE SEA

UNEI

ALAYSIA

NORTH PACIFIC OCEAN

INDONESIA

PAPUA
NEW
GUINEA

AUSTRALIA

FOLLOW TOM'S JOURNEY
AS YOU READ THE STORY...

Chapter 1

The pirate boat rolled easily in the swell pushing up from the South China Sea. It was past midnight. Overhead, the moon played hide and seek amongst the thunderclouds that towered ten thousand metres into the Malaysian night. To the south, towards Singapore, lightning flickered erratically, like a failing neon sign.

The wind was fitful. It blew in hot, uneven gusts over the mountains of Sumatra then down across the Malacca Straits. Small, steep-sided waves raced towards the mangrove swamps on the far side and broke with a ragged crash, amongst the millions of twisted roots.

The moon appeared and poured through a gap in the clouds, turning the sea into a sheet of silver foil. Lin Pao was the first to see the yacht. He caught the sudden flicker of movement as her sails shivered then filled again, as the squall raced past. The next moment, the boat disappeared into the glare. Lin Pao smiled in triumph. No one else had spotted it.

He had heard the rumour from a friendly fisherman that a large, ocean-going yacht was on her way down through the Straits. And now he had found her. Despite his own boat's broken radar, he had known where to find his prey. His hunting instincts were as good as ever.

His low cry brought the rest of the crew to their feet. There were eight of them. All barefoot. Shoes were liable to slip even on modern steel decks. They wore ragged shorts and vests and each man had a blue cotton band knotted around his forehead. It was the colour Lin Pao had chosen to distinguish his crew from Duang's people, back at base.

He swung the wheel over and brought the bows round until they pointed to where the yacht had been. Carefully, he pushed open the throttle. The hull began to vibrate and the sound of the engine grew to a powerful rumble. But not yet loud enough to be heard on board the other boat.

The crew shaded their eyes against the moonlight. They stared ahead, past the heavy machine gun mounted in the bows, straining for any sign of the yacht. Silently, they nudged one another to show their pleasure. They were proud to be in Lin Pao's crew. They were the best. Lin Pao was the best skipper in the Family. Their boat was the best. Hadn't Lin Pao himself escaped in it when he had deserted from the Chinese People's Navy? They had named her *Ular Ular*, after the yellow-banded sea snakes that infested these waters. She was the fastest craft in the Straits.

One of the pirates cried out and held up an arm. He gestured urgently to one side. Lin Pao spun the wheel still further. As he did so, the moon went in and they stood balancing on tiptoe, waiting for their night vision to return. The crewmen clicked their teeth in frustration and peered into the night. Thunder boomed over the mountains in a slow, majestic roll. Then at last, someone yelled. Moments later, Lin Pao saw the yacht again.

She was about three miles ahead; a beautiful winged creature under full sail with a streak of white water at her bow. Lin Pao gave a grunt of pleasure. He would not lose her this time. *Ular Ular*'s engine note deepened and the water under her stern began to boil. The pirates felt the rush of wind on their faces and grinned at one another.

As they closed the gap, the crew studied the yacht with professional interest. She was keeping well over to the Malaysian side of the Straits, right at the edge of the shipping lane. Not far away, in the middle of the channel, a fully laden supertanker ploughed its way south, leaving a ten-metre-deep furrow in its wake. Lin Pao kept half an eye on the tanker's navigation lights, watching for any change of course. A hole in the sea that size spelt certain disaster for any yacht that fell into it. And that included the *Ular Ular*. Both boats would be swamped in minutes, reduced to waterlogged hulks, waiting to be run down by the next ship that came along. And out here, the supertankers followed each other, like a herd of elephants.

The yacht was now much closer and clearly visible. The moonlight glinted on stainless steel winches and carbon fibre masts, as she soared gracefully over the swell. She was an ocean-going boat, a good twenty metres in length. She had a main cabin forward and a smaller one behind a roomy open cockpit. She looked beautiful and expensive. Lin Pao's crew murmured in anticipation.

'She's making six knots,' Lin Pao told them. He looked over to the Sumatran side, gauging the strength of the wind. Sheet lightning glowed pink and green deep inside the clouds massed above the mountains. There was a storm coming. He could smell it on the wind. All the more reason to close quickly.

'She'll stay steady on this tack,' he called. 'We'll be up with her in five minutes. You know what to do!'

The crew licked their lips and fingered the knives at their belts.

Lin Pao turned and looked back over his shoulder. For some moments, he stared intently, checking to make sure they were not being followed. Some months ago, the Malaysian authorities had announced a crackdown on pirates. In the weeks that followed, they had flooded the Straits with warships. Whenever Lin Pao thought he had spotted one on the radar, he had taken evasive action and hidden behind one of the hundreds of small islands that dotted the Straits.

Satisfied there was nothing behind him now, he concentrated on the job in hand. It was time to attack. He eased the throttle and the bows slowly sank.

'We'll come in starboard side!' he called in a low voice. 'So get ready. All of you! And No Noise!'

Some pirate captains liked to circle their victims, firing warning shots from rifles or machine guns until they surrendered. Duang, his great rival, was one of these. The thought of Duang made Lin Pao instinctively spit over the side. 'Cowboy,' he muttered, as he brought the *Ular Ular* to within a hundred metres of the yacht's stern. For Lin Pao, the essential element of any attack was surprise. No matter how big the other vessel was. And that meant getting as many men as possible on board the victim before anyone there realized what was happening.

Fifty metres behind the yacht, Lin Pao cut the engines. The *Ular Ular*'s momentum would bring them level within the next minute. Now, the only sound to be heard was the slap of sea on the hull and the creak of rigging from the yacht in front. Seconds later, he could see the glow of instruments from the yacht's cockpit. He took a deep breath and checked his crew. They stood waiting, their bodies tensed for action. The man at either end of the boat began to swing his steel grappling-hook.

There was music playing from somewhere inside the yacht. The thump of the bass grew louder. It drowned out all noise as the *Ular Ular* closed the gap like a cat gathering to pounce. As her bow drew level with the yacht's stern, Lin Pao raised a clenched fist.

There was a sudden flash of light. Lin Pao jerked his head away, momentarily blinded. Now voices and the sound of laughter filled the cockpit. Instinctively, he brought the wheel hard over and yanked open the throttle for a fierce burst of power.

'Throw!' he screamed.

The grappling-hooks snaked across. It was a simple throw and the men were experts. The hooks caught in the yacht's deck gear and held fast. The pirates whipped the ropes around cleats in the deck and physically heaved the boats together.

There was a long, screeching crash. *Ular Ular*'s deck tilted hard over and the night was suddenly full of thrashing sails. There was a rush of bodies and the next moment screams and confused shouting. Lin Pao stepped over the yacht's guardrail and threw himself to one side as the boom swung towards him. It smashed against the *Ular Ular*'s bridge and split wide open. Bending low, he hurried towards the cockpit.

He took the steps down into the main cabin at a jump. Inside, his men were already hard at work. He landed easily and immediately sensed the thickness of the carpet under his feet. A quick glance around took in the mahogany chart table and the array of radio and navigational equipment above it. The yacht was brand new.

He saw three Europeans huddled together at the far end of the salon. An older man was crouched on one knee, moaning loudly. He held his head in both hands. Blood was welling up between his fingers and running down his arm. The cotton T-shirt he was wearing was already badly stained. Lin Pao thought he was about sixty.

A woman had her arms around his shoulders, holding him to her, comforting him. Lin Pao saw the sparkle from the square diamond ring she was wearing. It was hard to miss. She looked up at him, her eyes wide in terror, and saw Lin Pao looking her. She screamed and buried her face in the man's neck. Lin Pao knew she was the sort of woman who would have a lot more rings.

The other man was much younger. Tall, ashen-faced and wearing glasses. Their son, perhaps? Lin Pao hoped so. It would simplify matters. There were tumblers on the cabin table and a half-full bottle of good brandy.

'Get the woman out of it!' Lin Pao ordered.

Chou, the bosun, reached down and yanked the woman to her feet. She screamed and began to flail at him with her fists. The bosun slapped her once across the face then pushed her away. The woman's screaming stopped and she began to sob instead. The younger man stood in front of her, trying to shield her. Everyone looked at Lin Pao.

For twenty seconds he said nothing, until the tension grew unbearable. Then he spoke in halting

8

English. 'I want your money, your watches, jewellery, drugs, ship's papers, passports. You have three minutes to find everything. Or this man dies.' He jabbed a finger at the younger man. 'You die!'

Then, to Chou the bosun, 'Get the safe open! The old man will have the key.'

Lin Pao turned and left them and went through into the rear salon. Two of his men were checking the boat's supplies, picking out the most attractive items.

'I want to be out of here in five minutes,' he told them.

He went up into the cockpit and looked around. The sea was splashing up between the two boats leaving wet patches on the yacht's wooden deck. He called to the lookout on board the *Ular Ular*.

'Nothing happening,' the man told him.

'Well, keep a damn good lookout just the same!' growled Lin Pao.

Back in the main cabin, the older white man was standing by an empty safe. His hands and arms were shaking uncontrollably. On the chart table, there was a pile of valuables. Lin Pao turned them over then began stuffing the bundles of bank-notes and traveller's cheques into the pockets of his old navy jacket. He picked up a small velvet pouch and weighed it in the palm of his hand. He pulled open the draw strings and looked inside. He couldn't help smiling. He was right. The woman was a walking jewellery store.

Not a bad haul, he thought. Twenty thousand American dollars for a start. And all that jewellery on top. But there was more. The Europeans were each carrying two passports. One British and the other Australian. Lin Pao knew that genuine passports were worth their weight in gold to the shadowy Dragon Family bosses, over on the Malaysian mainland. The Family had many interests. Piracy was only one of them. He had never met any of the big bosses from the mainland. There was no reason why he should have. He was only a humble pirate captain. But this haul would do him no harm back at his own base. The Dragon Lady for one, would surely be pleased. And it was about time she started treating him with proper respect. He was by far her best captain. Much better than that idiot Duang.

Lin Pao reached over the table, took the brandy bottle and poured out two generous tots. He gave one to Chou. Then, mockingly, he raised his glass towards the Europeans. He downed his drink in one gulp and turned to go. The woman's ring glinted as she clutched her husband's shoulder.

Lin Pao stared at her in disbelief, his face darkening in rage.

'The ring! She's still wearing her ring!' He kicked the nearest pirate. 'Get it off her, you fool!'

Chou shouldered the man aside and grabbed the woman's hand. He began to twist the ring off. But the woman was terrified and her finger had swollen.

'Try soap or cooking oil!' Lin Pao ordered. 'And if that doesn't work, use your knife!'

He pushed his way towards the radio transmitter bolted to a bulkhead. He drew out a pistol, put the muzzle against the control panel and fired. In the confines of the cabin, the noise was shocking.

By the time the crew of the yacht realized the pirates had gone, *Ular Ular* was a mile away and moving fast. For a long time afterwards, the woman sat unmoving, staring in disbelief at the blood-soaked bandage on her left hand.

Back on his own bridge, Lin Pao listened to the sound of spray splattering against the glass windscreen. The wind was getting up and the sea was growing lumpy. Chou stood beside him drinking tea from a stained mug.

Lin Pao looked at him. 'What happened to the woman's finger?'

Chou laughed. 'I put it back in the brandy bottle!'

Chapter 2

'Come on, Tom!' Mrs Lee called from the kitchen. 'Breakfast's on the table and we've a lot to do today!'

Tom Lee lay in bed and considered. Tomorrow evening, he'd be boarding a long-distance bus and driving the four hundred and fifty miles to Singapore. And the day after that, he'd be meeting his dad's ship when it docked. Then he'd be sailing back home to Penang with him. He grinned. He had wanted to go to sea for as long as he could remember. Now, he was going to do it on a proper ship.

'I'm putting your eggs on!'

His mother was dead right, though. There was loads to do. Like packing. Like taking the ferry over to the mainland and picking up his pre-booked ticket. That would save time tomorrow. There was always a long queue at the bus station for the coach to Singapore.

Most importantly, he mustn't forget his passport. His father had told him he needed to show it at the border. He had never had a passport before.

'Tom! I'm not telling you again!'

He gave a loud yawn and kicked off the sheet. He switched on the bedside radio. A reporter in a helicopter was describing heavy traffic on the Harbour Bridge coming on to Penang Island. There was no problem with the ferry service, though. It was still running as usual. Good.

Sunlight streamed in through the thin cotton curtains. It was going to be another hot day. Nothing unusual in that, of course. It was only during the monsoon months that the sun disappeared for days at a time.

Tom poked his head out of the window. The Lees' bungalow was old and made of wood. It was one of several perched on a low hill overlooking a market. The market was already in full swing. Women in brightly coloured head scarves sat beside palm mats heaped with red and green chillis, purple aubergines, bananas, mangoes, ladies' fingers and vegetables Tom didn't even know the names of.

Other stalls sold clothes, shoes, cooking pots and plastic toys. Office workers were stopping to buy sticky cakes and cups of sweet tea before scanning their morning newspapers. Cars and bicycles threaded their way through the stream of bustling humanity. Tom grinned. It was a cheerful, happy scene and it matched his mood perfectly.

The bathroom door wouldn't close properly. It was flimsy and had begun to warp. His father had hung it on his last shore leave. That was four months ago. Since then, he had been promoted and now had command of his own ship.

'She's the *Serota Star*,' he had told them on the telephone from Bangkok. 'The oldest boat in the Line. No one else wants her!'

The boy smiled. He was no psychologist but even he could hear the pride in his father's voice. His dad was all right, Tom thought. His mother told him that the bosses of the South Asia Shipping Lines must think very highly of him, because he was young to have command of his own ship. Since then, he had taken a cargo of television sets to New York and brought back a thousand ice-making machines for unloading in Dubai.

Tom filled a basin with lukewarm water and splashed it over his face. Then he cleaned his teeth. He looked in the mirror as he finished. His hair stood up in a series of damp spikes. He ran a comb through a couple of times, then used his hand to flatten them. He was only partially successful.

He was a stocky boy of thirteen. He had friendly black eyes and a ready grin. He was a promising swimmer and, last term, had started doing judo. He had only one ambition and that was to go to sea. Ships and engines of all types fascinated him. He spent most of his free time hanging round the fishing harbour or helping out in the garage at the bottom of the road.

His mother talked enthusiastically about his becoming a doctor or an accountant and she was really pushy about school exams. Tom said nothing. He knew what he was going to do and had done so for years. He was going to join South Asia Shipping as a deck cadet the minute he turned seventeen. And that was that!

'Tom, this egg's going to be hard boiled!'

'Coming, Ma!' he shouted.

As he hurried into the kitchen, his mother's pet parrot put its head to one side and looked at him. Then it screamed and began tugging at the bars of its cage.

'Stop that!' Mrs Lee snapped. 'Or I'll put your cover back on.'

The parrot screeched loudly and hopped off its

perch. It began scratching in the sand at the bottom of the cage.

'I don't know what's got into him,' she complained, putting a plate in front of Tom. 'Perhaps he knows you're going away.' She spooned the egg out of a saucepan and into an eggcup. 'They do say birds can sense things coming.'

Tom shook his head. 'That's only earthquakes or tsunamis and things. Not people going away. Not for personal things.'

A woman appeared at the open kitchen door. She was Mrs Wen from next door. She was older than his mother and lived on her own. Tom thought she was a rather sad person. She seemed to have no other friends and talked a great deal.

She beamed at them, put her bag on the kitchen table and began rummaging around in it. Tom moved his plate to one side. Triumphantly, she pulled out a large bar of pink and white coloured coconut ice. She must have bought it that morning in the market. He could see her thumbprint as she handed it to him.

'This is for our brave traveller,' she smiled. 'To keep up his strength for the long journey.'

Tom smiled at her. 'Thank you!' he said and went back to scraping out the last of his egg.

'I won't stay long because I know you must be busy,' she told them shyly. 'Oh well then! I'd love a cup of tea. How kind.'

'Are you sure you wouldn't like me to take Tom to the ferry tomorrow?' she asked. 'It's no trouble, you know. It's going to be an emotional time for you.'

His mother laughed and shook her head. 'He's only going to be away for a few days. He'll be home by the weekend. Hardly seems worth his while.' And she winked at her son.

'Wish I was going on with the ship to England,' Tom put in.

'And leave your mother all on her own!' Mrs Wen sounded rather shocked. 'Is he being met?' she went on. 'Only Singapore's such a huge place and one does hear stories.'

Mrs Lee frowned. 'The ship's agent's going to be there. A Mrs Chung. Her husband's a police sergeant.'

Mrs Wen looked happier. 'I do envy you, Tom. I hope it's not costing too much?'

'No! It's free,' Mrs Lee told her. 'And the Company's delighted. Now you must excuse us,' she said firmly. 'We've got so much to do!'

'Well I'm sure Tom deserves it,' Mrs Wen said with a smile. 'And you should go yourself. See a bit of the world before it's too late.'

'Well done, Mum!' Tom said after she had gone. 'She'd talk the hind leg off a donkey, if you let her.'

His mother shrugged. 'She's lonely, Tom. And she is a neighbour.' She clattered the plates and put them in the sink. 'Besides, there are plenty worse people in the world than Mrs Wen. You'll find that out one of these days!'

Then she smiled. 'Time you got packed. Shall we make a start?'

Chapter 3

In an office at the back of a run-down building in the poorest part of town, a fax machine began to chatter. Moments later a sheet of paper fell to the floor and joined the others lying there.

At the same time, a taxi pulled up in the street outside. Although it was still early in the morning, the air was already full of dust and the stink of exhaust fumes. A nondescript dog scrambled to its feet and limped out of the way. It had a paw missing. Flies buzzed around a sore on the side of its head. A small boy appeared from an alleyway, saw it and chased after it. He carried a stick.

A heavily-built man clambered out of the car. He wore a faded cotton suit and a pair of scuffed black shoes. There were sweat marks at the armpits and his trousers were just a little too short. He looked as if he might have been a boxer or a stevedore. Something like that. He was in fact an ex-member of the French Foreign Legion. Somewhere in the Defence Ministry in Paris, there was a file on him with the word 'Deserter' under his faded photograph. But that was all twenty years in the past.

He reached into a back pocket and pulled out a bundle of greasy bank-notes. Carefully, he counted out the fare and added a tip. The driver thanked him and drove off. The man mopped his face with a large silk handkerchief then turned and began to climb a flight of worn stairs towards a large open door. The sign beside the door read 'George Patou – Import/Export'. On the wall beside it were the faded words 'Fat French Pig', spray-painted in Malay.

Mr Patou always smiled when he saw this graffiti. For some reason, which no one dared ask, the insult amused him and he refused to have it painted over. It had been put there a year ago by the husband of a disgruntled employee. The man had afterwards been found with a shattered knee. He was a beggar now, with one hand held out for small change and the other holding on to a wooden crutch. The woman was long gone.

He strode into the workshop and made his way

between rows of small tables. The foreman rushed to meet him, smiling expansively to show off his new gold tooth. The thirty women sitting at the sewing-machines bent their heads and concentrated on cutting and stitching the soft toys they were busy making for the American Christmas market. A radio was playing local pop music. The wailing of the singer could just be heard above the buzz of activity.

Mr Patou cast an expert eye over the room. He noted the full boxes piled up along the walls and the bales of fresh cloth beside each woman. He listened to the foreman's report then dismissed him with a nod and walked briskly towards his office. He undid the locks and went inside.

His first act was to go over to the fax machine where he stooped and gathered up the waiting sheets of paper. For a big man, his movements were surprisingly nimble. He fanned through them. At the third one, he gave a grunt. He looked back towards the open door. A woman was approaching holding a cup of tea. Not now! He swung his leg and kicked the door shut. He heard her cry of surprise and ignored it. He put the fax down carefully in the middle of his desk, went to an old-fashioned steel safe and spun the dial. When it was open, he reached in and drew out a stack of folders. He flicked through them until he found the one he wanted.

There was the logo of a well-known shipping company on the front cover and the words 'Very Secret. Chief Executive Eyes Only' were stamped underneath in large red letters. There was also a warning that any unauthorized use would result in criminal prosecution. Inside, there were a dozen pages covered in neatly printed columns of letters and numbers.

For the next half-hour, Mr Patou methodically decoded the numbers from the fax on to a note-pad. With rising excitement, he double-checked the information. Drops of sweat trickled down his neck and the fax paper curled under his hand. His collar was becoming much too tight. He wrenched it open. The telephone rang four times but he did not notice it.

Abruptly, he stood up. His chair fell over with a bang. He snatched a calendar from the wall behind his desk. His eyes darted over it, tracing the dates with a sausage-like forefinger. He puffed out his cheeks and gave a wheeze of excitement.

This was the big one! The one he had spent years waiting for but never really believing it might happen. Why, with his share of the proceeds, he might even be able to retire and live somewhere nice. If they'd let him! His chest felt suddenly tight and he had to clutch the side of the desk. He reached in a drawer for a brown plastic bottle and put two pills in his mouth. He stood there and waited for his heart to stop racing.

He had to get the information to them right away. It was going to be touch and go as it was. There was hardly any time to put it all together. But that wasn't his problem. Thank God! But he must tell them. That was his job. If they missed out because of him, he'd be dead in the water. Literally.

His hands shook as he reached for the telephone. He could feel more sweat gathering in his armpits. The call took no more than ten seconds to make. The voice at the other end was cold and unemotional.

'Usual place! In one hour. You better be right!'

Mr Patou grabbed his note-pad and scanned it. His heart was thumping again. Like a steam hammer this time. What if he'd got it wrong? What if he'd misread something? What if? He thrust the thought from him. After all, he had been a corporal in the Legion. A better man than any of them would ever be. He stuffed the pad into a pocket and strode through the hum of the workshop, into the brilliant day outside.

Chapter 4

Tom shifted in his seat and tried to get comfortable. A couple of minutes later, he had to turn around again. He had been sitting in the coach for almost seven hours and his bottom was numb. His eyes felt gritty and there was a nasty taste in his mouth. He had never been so bored in all his life with nothing to see and nothing to do. The only excitement, if you could call it that, was the occasional flash of headlights from an oncoming vehicle. He wondered how the driver managed to stay awake.

All around him, other people slept or sat motionless in the darkness. Occasionally, someone coughed or cried out in their sleep. Here and there, an overhead light was switched on or off. And always, there was the endless drumming of tyres on the road.

He rested his head against the window and closed

his eyes. If only he could get back to sleep. He knew he had been asleep earlier, before the bus had stopped at the last small town. He had been woken by people clambering on to the bus and pushing their bags into overhead lockers. Outside, in the glow of oil lamps, there had been stalls serving food. The air was heavy with the scent of sizzling duck and vegetables and smoke from the charcoal fires. That was when the man beside him had got on. Tom didn't like him very much. He had bad breath and slept with his mouth wide open.

The coach gave a lurch and Tom's head banged against the window. Furious, he flung himself around in his seat. His foot kicked the man's ankle and he woke up, spluttering with anger.

'Keep still! Damn you! Or go and sit elsewhere. You're worse than a dog with fleas!' He turned his back on Tom and cleared his throat, loudly.

Tom made a face at the man's back. Well, that solved the bad breath problem for the time being, he thought. He closed his eyes and slumped down. He thought about home and his mother. She had told him she was looking forward to seeing both her 'men' next weekend but in the meantime she was going to have a well-deserved rest. He smiled. Some hope, knowing her!

He imagined himself on his father's ship, doing all sorts of amazing things. He discovered a fire in the engine room and single-handedly put it out. He steered the ship away in the nick of time from a wicked-looking reef. Soon afterwards, he was being offered his own ship to command.

He enjoyed the daydream for a little longer until a genuine worry brought him back to earth. He was supposed to be met by a Mrs Chung, the ship's agent, when he reached Singapore. His father thought the world of her. Tom remembered him saying, 'That Mrs Chung's a real superwoman! Whatever you need, she'll have it there waiting on the dockside for you. She keeps the whole Line afloat!'

Tom had never met her and had no idea what she looked like. His mother thought she wasn't very tall but then there were a lot of people like that. What if she wasn't there to meet him? Or if they missed each other in the crush of people? His mother had written her telephone number down for him on a piece of paper. The only trouble was he had forgotten where he had put it. He yawned. The engine note deepened and the noise of the tyres was becoming much quieter. Without expecting to, Tom fell sound asleep.

He woke with a start as the man with bad breath

gave him a sharp dig in the ribs.

'Singapore!' he huffed. 'Now you can scratch again.' And he laughed.

Tom scowled and sat up. He looked out of the window and gasped. They were driving along a wide highway lined with smart, white-painted apartment blocks. They all seemed to be over twenty storeys in height and stretched away on either side of the road, as far as he could see. In between, there were clumps of elegant palm trees and neatly mown grass lawns. It looked like a huge film set.

The customs building was air-conditioned and very clean. Going through customs was no problem. Tom's hand shook slightly as he handed his passport to an unsmiling official. The man stamped it, turned in his seat and waved at someone. He handed the passport back.

'Welcome to Singapore. There's a lady waiting to meet you.'

Tom grinned at the man and walked past. He heard his name called and scanned the crowd behind the barrier several times before he spotted a very small woman waving at him. She disappeared behind a couple of backpackers then re-emerged with a beaming smile.

'Tom!' she cried. 'I'm Doris Chung. Good to meet you!' She shook hands energetically. 'Here! Let me help you with that.'

And before he could stop her, she had seized his bag and was hurrying away with it. Tom scuttled after her feeling dazed. She was a human dynamo and Billy Whizz all rolled into one. That bag was heavy! Outside, she led the way to a battered Volkswagen beetle and dumped his bag on the back seat. She caught him staring at a long scrape down one side.

'I'm not a good driver,' she told him. 'Too impatient!' She laughed and reversed rapidly out of the parking slot. Five minutes later, they were driving in fast traffic along another large highway. 'Morning rush hour!' she informed him.

Tom nodded and studied her from the corner of his eye. She was perched on a thick cushion on top of the driver's seat. Even so, her head barely showed above the steering wheel. On either side of them, trucks and buses thundered along.

'You must be tired!' she called, looking across at him.

'A little bit. Yes.'

A truck horn blasted from somewhere high above them. Tom blinked.

'Here's what we'll do,' she told him. 'I'll take you

back to our flat. Give you some breakfast. Then, I must go to work. You can sleep till lunch-time. My husband will take you out for lunch.

'We've got a problem with your father's ship,' Mrs Chung began to say, then gave an exclamation. In front of them, a van braked hard. She swerved to avoid it. The car behind flashed its lights.

'What's wrong?' he gasped. 'Is it serious?'

Mrs Chung shook her head. 'Nothing wrong with the *Serota Star*. She may be old but she's reliable. And South Asia Lines do a good job looking after their ships. Much better than most. No! Your dad's having trouble with the radio. I've got to get some new parts,' she added. 'And have them fitted. I'm trying to fix everything before they dock this afternoon.'

She drummed her fingers on the steering wheel. 'Trouble is the ship's only in for oil bunkering, so we haven't got much time. You know what bunkering is?'

'It's when they refuel a ship.'

Mrs Chung nodded. 'Good. The problem is she must be on her way by midday tomorrow at the latest. She's got a big cargo. And I'm having problems getting one of the radio parts.'

She pointed to a huge overhead road sign coming up ahead. 'This is where we come off. Sit tight!'

They threaded their way across the streams of traffic. Tom stared straight ahead while high-sided vehicles roared past on both sides. Somehow, they reached the slip road and pulled off in time.

Mrs Chung saw his face and laughed. 'That was easy. Some days it's quite frightening! Anyway, it's nice and slow from now on.'

They were soon driving at a snail's pace through narrow streets and a crush of people. Bicycles were everywhere, many overloaded with bulging sacks slung over their crossbars. There were rickshaws powered by little two-stroke engines and lorries belching clouds of black exhaust. Metre-deep monsoon ditches ran along the sides of the road. There were shops and stalls and street vendors. The noise was deafening.

'What does Sergeant Chung do? I mean what sort of policeman is he?'

Mrs Chung shrugged. 'Why don't you ask him when you see him?' She pointed to a low-rise block of flats. 'Here we are. Home sweet home. Let's get you in.'

Chapter 5

A flock of parrots landed in the treetops high above the landing-stage. They disturbed a family of monkeys already feeding there. For a few moments, the stillness of the afternoon was broken by angry screechings. Then the parrots rose in a cloud of brilliant reds and blues and flew back across the river, protesting shrilly to one another. Far below, a sea snake meandered past the old wooden jetty and made its leisurely way down the side of the *Ular Ular*.

Two pirate boats were tied up on either side and hidden from view under the canopy of trees. At the far end of the pier, a cluster of huts could be seen. To a casual observer, it resembled a typical fishing village. A number of small boats were pulled up above the high-water mark. Another was in the process of being built. New planks lay beside it on the grass. A man was sitting out in the open repairing a net. In a few hours' time, smoke would start rising from the thatched roofs, as the womenfolk began to prepare the evening meal.

A boy sat cross-legged beside the path. He was cleaning the *Ular Ular*'s machine gun. The gun itself had been broken down into a dozen parts and laid out neatly on a length of old sacking. Duc To hummed tunelessly to himself and wondered how many times he had cleaned the gun.

Two hundred? More like double that, he decided. Still, it was better than working in the cookhouse. Anything was better than that. He looked around hoping to see his friend Nancy. She must still be up at the big house looking after that evil old woman. He shivered and bent his head over his work.

Nancy kept him sane. She was calm and sensible and without her, Duc To knew, he would have bolted into the jungle ages ago. Someone had tried to escape the day after he had been brought here. The pirates had found the body. Snakebite, he remembered hearing someone say. They had left it for the rats and insects to pick clean.

The boy sighed and wiped an oily rag along the gun barrel. Rust could form within an hour in this climate and the punishment for allowing that to happen was two days and nights in the punishment cage. The thought depressed him still further. If only Nancy would come. She always cheered him up. She was his only friend and he loved her fiercely.

After three years, he didn't remember much about his own family in Vietnam. If he shut his eyes and concentrated hard, he could just make out his mother's face. But it was an effort. His father was dead. He had seen the pirates throw him overboard together with his two elder brothers. When he had asked Nancy why they had spared him, she had laughed and told him they needed child slaves to do their chores. After all, she had been waiting on the old woman and taking up her food ever since he had known her. A hand ruffled his hair. Nancy!

'How you doing?' she demanded, squatting down beside him. She was small and lithe with jet-black hair that reached her waist. She wore a faded cotton dress and was barefoot.

'Getting there!' he grinned. He picked up the wooden cleaning rod and screwed the phosphor-bronze brush back in place. Then he pushed it up and down inside the barrel a couple more times. Next, he put the barrel to his eye. The inside shone a burnished blue. He grunted in satisfaction. It was immaculate.

'Finished?' she demanded. 'Good! Let's go down to the fish traps. I want a walk. There's time, isn't there?' She started getting to her feet.

Duc To pulled her back down. 'I'm waiting for Chou to come and inspect.'

Nancy screwed up her face. 'I hate Chou. He killed my mum and dad.' And she spat as hard as she could.

The boy studied her. 'Had a bad morning?'

Nancy nodded. 'SHE's in one of her moods. So everyone's walking round on eggshells.' Nancy jerked her thumb towards the line of steps that led up the side of the hill. 'SHE wants both boats out tonight. But Duang's got a problem with his electrics.'

Duc To gave a short laugh. 'Duang's always got a problem. His boat's a disaster area.'

She shrugged. 'You're right. But I prefer him to Chou or Lin Pao. He's a bit more friendly.'

'That's the same as the difference between a python and a cobra. They'll both kill you if you don't look out!'

She nudged him sharply. 'Chou's coming!'

The boy busied himself until Chou was standing in front of him. Then he scrambled up and stood waiting nervously.

Chou picked the barrel up with both hands and held it towards the sky. With one eye closed he squinted up inside. There was a brief pause. Then, 'Call this clean?' he sneered. 'You could grow rice in there! It's filthy!'

He tossed the barrel back. Duc To threw up his hands to protect his face and caught it clumsily. 'Get it clean! I'll be back in twenty minutes! D'you hear?'

The boy stared at the ground. 'Yes, sir!'

Chou considered him. 'How old are you, Duc To?'

The boy looked surprised. 'Twelve, I think.'

'And how long have you been here?'

'Three years, sir.'

Chou shook his head. 'So! We save your life. We feed you. Give you some responsibility. And this is how you repay us.' His face darkened. 'We should have got rid of you as well. You're all the same, you Vietnamese,' he hissed. 'Good for nothing!' And slapped him across the face.

Nancy stepped in front of Duc To, pushing him away. 'And you're just a bully!'

Chou blinked in surprise then laughed out loud. 'Listen to her!' He stooped over the girl and brought his face very close to hers. 'Just because you work for the Dragon Lady, don't you start getting any fancy ideas. You're a nobody! See! Never forget it. We can replace you just like that!' And he clicked his fingers.

They watched Chou walk on towards the village. 'One day I'll kill him,' she said.

'Dream on, Nancy,' the boy said bitterly. 'There's nothing we can do. 'There's no way out of here for either of us.'

Chapter 6

Mr Patou sat with his back to the wall and watched a waiter wipe a dirty cloth over the bar counter. He always sat facing into a room like this. It was a trick he had learnt as a young soldier amongst the seedy taverns and dance halls of Marseilles. He needed to watch the comings and goings of people. Who came in. Whom they left with. He liked to see people's hands. Especially if they were keen to keep them out of sight. After twenty years of doing business in the Far East, this obsession had probably saved his life on at least three occasions.

He picked up his glass and slowly drained it. He pushed back the cuff of his jacket and peered at his watch. It wasn't easy to see in the pink overhead lighting. The man was a whole hour late! Mr Patou could imagine the fuss there'd be if he turned up an hour late for a meeting! Angrily, he clicked his fingers and held up his glass. The barman came over with a fresh bottle.

Although it was only mid-morning, the atmosphere in 'Garry's Bar' was already smoky. Two American sailors were slumped at a nearby table, their heads almost touching. There was an overflowing ashtray beside each of them. The club bouncer sat at the bar trying to read the local sports page. From time to time, he looked across at the sailors.

Quite suddenly Mr Patou's contact was in the room. He had long bony hands and moved like a cat. Even Patou had not seen him enter. One moment he was not there. The next, he was sitting down beside him. The man barked an order at the barman. The radio was turned up loud.

'You're late,' Mr Patou grumbled. 'What kept you?'

'Business. What else?'

Patou glared at him. He noticed the bulge in the front of the man's jacket. Not his concern of course. He sighed inwardly and wished for the thousandth time that he could end his dealings with these people. But he needed them and the protection they offered. They, apparently, still valued his own contacts and business cover.

'So? Tell me!' the man demanded. His voice was hard. Unemotional.

Mr Patou took a deep breath. 'There's a ship with a cargo worth twenty million American dollars coming in here for repairs, this afternoon.' He looked at his watch, with an exaggerated flourish. 'In four hours' time, to be exact.'

He studied the man's face, looking for any reaction. There was none. No thanks. No congratulations. No excitement. Nothing.

'What sort of cargo?'

Mr Patou stared at him in disbelief. For a fleeting moment, his fists bunched. He'd just love to 'stick it' to the man. Anything to knock that deadpan expression from his little weasel face. Just the once. Which was all it would be, of course. After that, the police would be fishing his headless body out of the harbour. Instead, he took a deep breath and held himself back. He leant forward conspiratorally.

'Consumer goods. Plasma TVs. The latest video games; media players,' he enthused. 'It's twenty per cent of the entire Subishi Corporation's Christmas exports to the UK!'

One of the sailors had sat up and was shouting for a drink. Patou heard the aggression thickening in his voice. The barman turned his back and ignored him. The sailor picked up an empty bottle and hurled it. It exploded with a sharp crack against a wall. Pieces of glass flew everywhere. The other sailor, jerked into sudden consciousness by the noise, got to his feet. He stood there swaying gently then staggered towards the bar. He stumbled and tried to hang on to a table, and yelled as his hands gripped the broken glass. He fell heavily, bringing a chair down with him.

Patou and his contact watched in silence as the bouncer went to work. It was not pretty and it didn't take long. The bouncer was soon back holding a wallet. He pulled out a couple of bank-notes. He handed the barman one and put the other in his trouser pocket.

The man beside Mr Patou called him over. He held out his hand for the wallet. He took out the sailor's identity card then gave the wallet back to the bouncer. The barman swept up the pieces of glass and life returned to normal.

'Well?' demanded Patou. 'Are you interested or not!'

The man looked at him with cold eyes. 'Name of ship?'

Mr Patou hesitated. Grief! Had his memory gone blank? Then he remembered with a rush. '*Serota Star*. South Asia Lines.'

'What repairs?'

Patou shrugged. 'New radio parts. They want to be ready to leave midday tomorrow.'

The weasel man flicked his fingers. 'Give me their fax.'

He read it in silence, frowning over the meaning of some of the words. Eventually he said, 'The Chung woman is buying the parts they need?'

'And getting the technician to fit them.' Mr Patou nodded.

'Not much time,' the other observed.

Mr Patou threw up his hands in despair. 'I told you it was urgent. I wasn't making it up!' He thought for a moment longer. And had a brain-wave. 'Why don't your people install some sort of tracking device on board the ship? I don't know if they make such things but it'd be worth finding out? Wouldn't it?'

The man stood up. 'Not your problem. You do your job. We do ours. Not your business!'

Mr Patou watched him go. He sat on for a few minutes longer, going over their conversation in his mind. That 'tracking' idea of his was brilliant. He couldn't think why he had never thought of it before. There must be ways of tracking ships electronically, or whatever the expression was, in this day and age. The least the man could have done was to have said thank you. Miserable little so and so.

Chapter 7

Someone was tugging at his shoulder. Pulling him up into the sunshine where he didn't want to be. Tom opened his eyes. A man was bending over him.

'Hello! I'm Sergeant Chung.'

Tom sat up hurriedly then clutched at his arm. 'Pins and needles,' he gasped.

The man looked sympathetic. 'Take your time. Try rubbing it gently.'

Sergeant Chung was tall and very thin. Like a beanpole, Tom thought. He imagined him beside Mrs Chung and couldn't help smiling. He got to his feet and shook hands.

'Feeling better?' asked Sergeant Chung. 'Good! Now it's time we went for lunch.'

Soon they were sitting at a table in the sunshine studying the menu.

'That's what I'd have if I was you,' said Sergeant Chung, pointing. 'Number fifty-four. With boiled rice. It's a local fish in a special shrimp sauce. It's what I eat whenever I come here.'

Tom nodded enthusiastically. Next, Sergeant Chung recommended the apple in toffee. He ordered a pot of green tea for himself. 'We've got half an hour,' he told Tom, glancing at his watch. 'Then we must be leaving. We'll get a cab down to Keppel Harbour. That's where the big ships dock.'

'Are you a detective?'

'Why would I be a detective?'

'Because you're in plain clothes.'

Sergeant Chung poured himself a cup of tea.

'In a way I am. Yes!' He lowered his voice. 'I work for an organization called SAPU. The State Anti-Piracy Unit.'

'Pirates!' Tom's eyes widened. 'Are you serious?'

It was Sergeant Chung's turn to look surprised. 'You mean your father hasn't told you? About these people, I mean?'

Tom shook his head. He stopped as a thought struck him. 'But I did hear something about them from some fishermen I know in Penang. It didn't seem to bother them too much.'

43

'That's because most pirates used to be fishermen themselves,' Sergeant Chung said dryly. He frowned. 'Well, I suppose you've a right to know. Seeing that you're going to be sailing slap bang through their back yard, so to speak.'

Tom stared at him.

Sergeant Chung poured himself another cup of tea and looked thoughtful. 'I'll try not to sound like a school teacher,' he said, 'but here are a few facts. The seas around Singapore and the Straits are the worst place in the world for pirates. We had over a hundred and fifty attacks last year.'

Tom's jaw dropped.

'The Malacca Straits,' Sergeant Chung went on, 'are the world's busiest waterway. Fifty thousand ships a year go through them. And there'll be a lot more in the future.'

'Because of China? And all those exports and things?'

The man nodded. 'Quite right! The Straits are like a huge motorway between Asia, the Middle East and Europe. Not to mention that almost all Japan's and China's oil supplies go through there too.'

Tom thought for a moment, trying to take this in. 'So where are all these pirates? I mean, where do they hang out?'

Sergeant Chung spread his hands. 'There are hundreds and hundreds of small islands in the Straits where they can hide or set up base. And then there're all the mangrove swamps and creeks. It's almost impossible to find them. And to make it worse,' he added, 'they use small boats with really fast engines. Very hard to see on radar.'

Tom shook his head. 'But how can they attack something as big as a tanker?'

'They come at night. They get really close to the rear of a ship, throw up grappling-hooks and climb on board. They're good seamen. Many of them were fishermen, as I was saying. They know what they're doing, believe me.'

'Then what? I mean, what happens when they get on board?'

Sergeant Chung made a face. 'They hold up the captain or the bridge watch keepers and force them to open the ship's safe. Mostly they just take money but sometimes they'll hijack an entire boat, if the cargo is valuable enough. That's when they murder the crew or throw them overboard for the sharks. They'll sail the ship to a Chinese port and sell the cargo there.'

'Well, I can't see my father letting a bunch of pirates take over his ship,' said Tom, hotly.

'Nor can I,' said Sergeant Chung. 'And it's time we went to meet him. Come on!'

Chapter 8

'Half ahead!' ordered Captain Lee.

'Half ahead it is,' repeated the helmsman, ringing the engine room telegraph.

'We've got to slow down to half speed through the Straits,' Captain Lee explained, turning to look for Tom, who was keeping out of the way at the back of the bridge.

The *Serota Star*'s wake stretched behind her like a ruler. The sun was almost directly overhead and it beat down with an intensity that made exposed metal surfaces painful to touch. The sea was a deep blue and the ship rolled easily in a gentle cross swell.

Tom's heart sang. He had never been so happy. Everything about the ship and of being at sea filled him with an intense joy. He was living in a dream which had started when his father had met him on top of the gangway yesterday.

'Good to see you, son!' Captain Lee had cried, shaking him by the hand. 'Welcome on board!' He had put an arm around Tom's shoulders and hugged him.

It was the first time Tom had seen his father wearing his captain's badges of rank. The four gold stripes gleamed brightly on the shoulders of his uniform shirt.

'See here, Tom,' his father had added. 'This is Robert, our steward. He'll take you to your cabin and show you over the ship. He'll bring you up to the bridge when we sail.'

He had looked across to Mrs Chung. 'Hello, Doris! Everything under control?'

'The spare parts are just arriving, Captain.' She indicated a white van on the dockside below. 'And I've hired the two best technicians in Singapore to fit them. Well, that's what I'm told they are!'

Captain Lee had bowed his head in relief. 'Well done! Thank you! Let's go to my cabin and start the paperwork.'

And now, thought Tom, here I am on the bridge of my dad's own ship. Brilliant!

'See that lighthouse, Tom?' Captain Lee broke in on his thoughts. 'About five miles dead ahead?'

Tom came forward and stood beside the man at the wheel. He nodded.

'That's the Horseburgh Light,' his father told him. 'It's where the Straits officially begin. And our headaches,' he added, looking around at the other people on the bridge. Someone laughed. 'Once you get into the Straits at this southern end, you're in a real bottle-neck.'

Tom looked at the expanse of water ahead and frowned. 'A bottle-neck?'

'Take another look at the chart!' Captain Lee explained. 'You see all those rocks and islands? Well, because of them, there are only eleven miles of sea room for everything to move about in. And as the Straits are divided into contraflows for ships coming from both directions at once, it's a bit like rush hour in Singapore. Give him the binoculars, someone.'

As Tom peered through the glasses, his father said, 'You should be able to see twelve ships coming towards us. Everything from a Russian trawler to a 500,000-ton Japanese supertanker. And if you look back over our stern, you'll find six more going the same way as us. If you can't find them, the officer of the watch will point them out to you on the radar screen.

Tom peered into the radar screen and saw two columns of greenish-coloured blobs. The blobs were actual ships and they flashed brightly whenever the radar beam passed over them.

'The nearest approaching ship is two miles away,' the watch keeper told him.

Tom gasped. 'But it looks so close! I can't believe it's that far!'

Captain Lee's voice cut in. He sounded alarmed. 'That first boat's turning! I don't believe it! Her skipper must have just woken up from his afternoon siesta.'

There was sudden tension on the bridge which grew with each passing minute. Tom watched engrossed, as his father strode between the radar plot and the captain's tall, fixed chair at the front of the bridge. The oncoming ship's bows had swung right around and Tom could now see down the other side of her hull.

'I don't believe it!' his father was still saying. 'The idiot's heading for that big refinery down there. This is going to be damn close!'

The officer of the watch bent over Tom and, speaking very quietly, explained. 'We're like a train running on fixed rails. We can't turn to starboard, to the right, because it gets shallow there very quickly. We'd soon be aground. We can't come much more to port, left-hand side, because we'll hit the next oncoming ship. And if we slow down, the ship behind will ram our stern. She's only a mile away.' He gave Tom a lopsided grin.

Tom took a deep breath and began to understand the worried faces all around. He took a look backwards through his glasses. An ore carrier was following them like a huge, lost dog. She was empty and riding high out of the water.

The officer of the watch saw him and murmured, 'She's the length of eleven soccer pitches, end to end. And at this speed, she'll take twelve miles to pull up.'

Tom puffed out his cheeks. He'd rather have not known that fact. Fascinated, he watched the approaching ship sail across in front of them. He thought he saw a face high up on her bridge but couldn't be sure. There was no one else in sight. She appeared to be deserted.

'It's going to be close, gentlemen,' growled Captain Lee, a few moments later. 'Too close! Sound the alarm bells!'

The turning ship filled the bridge windows. A door in her superstructure suddenly flew open and two men in cook's overalls emerged, carrying a dustbin. They looked up, saw the *Serota Star* and began shouting and gesticulating. Then they both bolted back inside like rabbits.

On board the *Serota Star*, alarm bells were ringing. Crewmen in life-jackets thudded up the stairways to take up positions by the lifeboats.

'Port ten degrees!' Captain Lee ordered abruptly. 'As quick as you can!'

He was rocking backwards and forwards on his heels. Tom saw his hands held rigidly behind his back, the fingers open. The ship in front blew a sudden deafening blast on her foghorn. For a moment, it stopped all coherent thought. Tom bit his tongue in shock and couldn't help crying out in pain.

'Three hundred metres . . . two . . .' his father called. 'We'll do it! We'll do it!'

The stern of the other ship seemed to be full of men waving their fists and shouting. They looked close enough to touch.

'I'll report him! God help me, I'll report him!' Captain Lee was shouting.

There was another blast from the foghorn. Now, Tom could see the pitted steel plates of her stern and her original name covered with many coats of paint. The water between the two ships surged up against their sides. Now, only twenty metres of boiling, milky-coloured ocean separated the two of them. And then they were sliding past. But only just!

A minute went by while normality returned. 'Stand down from action stations,' Captain Lee ordered in a normal voice. He put his hands on his head. 'That was the closest shave I've ever had,' he told them. There was a chorus of agreement. A telephone rang in the main console. The officer of the watch picked it up.

'Engineers want to know now the fun is over if they can start work on number two boat?'

Captain Lee sat down heavily in his chair and laughed. 'Affirmative.' He looked around. 'Tom! You need some fresh air. Can't stay cooped up in here all day. You can start earning your keep. Report to the engineers right away and learn all you can about boat engines. You never know when it might come in useful!'

A thought struck him. 'Oh and Tom,' he called. 'Go anywhere you want on board but whatever you do, do NOT fall overboard! Got it?'

Chapter 9

Lin Pao was in a filthy mood. The night before had not gone well. In fact, it could easily have ended in total disaster. He was mentally rehearsing the report he would give the Dragon Lady, in half an hour's time. She was not going to like it. Chou, the bosun, sat facing him on *Ular Ular*'s bridge. He held a mug of sweet tea in one scarred fist.

Lin Pao wondered if he looked as drained and tired as Chou did. His eyes felt raw and gritty and he had a searing headache. From stress, he imagined. The stink of cordite still clung to his hair and clothes. He no longer felt his usual, controlled self.

'We were lucky!' Chou told him, interrupting his thoughts. 'When that Navy boat appeared, I thought we were goners!'

'Let's go over the facts again,' snapped Lin Pao,

stealing a quick glance at his watch. He must not be late for the regular afternoon meeting with the Dragon Lady.

Chou took a slurp of tea. 'OK,' he said cheerfully. 'Let's see. We picked out a container ship, fifty miles north of here. Nothing fancy about her. Made a normal approach. Came up under her stern, all tickety-boo. Throttled back ready to board, when . . .'

'A searchlight came on,' Lin Pao interrupted, 'and blinded us.'

'And then all their crew turned out and began dropping damn great concrete blocks on top of us.' Chou shook his head. 'And that's never happened before, neither.'

Lin Pao closed his eyes, reliving the scream of the engine as he sheered away from the merchantman's towering hull.

'Gets worse,' Chou reminded him.

He sounded almost cheerful, Lin Pao thought sourly. Almost as if he was enjoying it. His mouth tightened. But the man was right about one thing. It had got worse!

Chou hawked and spat expertly over the side. 'Five minutes later we hit a rain squall. Blotted out everything. And of course, the radar's still not working. When we get clear, we're in the middle of a fishing fleet.'

Lin Pao remembered the panic. Himself at the wheel, weaving a frantic course in and out of the bobbing little boats. Praying the propeller would not snag one of their nets. And the truly heart-stopping moment when a Malaysian Navy patrol boat appeared out of the darkness, dead ahead of them.

'Bit of luck, then,' Chou reminded him. 'Good thing we had old Sam on the gun. He kept their heads down, all right!' He laughed.

Whether it had been pure luck or good shooting, Lin Pao couldn't decide. Sam, the *Ular*'s gunner, had fired first, a long burst of machine gun fire that raked the other's bridge. The *Ular Ular* had swept past, still pumping fire into the Navy boat, which made no attempt to follow.

'Gave her a right seeing to,' said the bosun with relish.

Lin Pao got to his feet. 'It means they'll put out a lot more patrols up there. And that's not going to make life easier for any of us.'

Chou scratched his nose. 'So we go south for a change. Besides, the government's not got that many boats. Cheer up, Lin Pao! We're still in one piece, you and me.'

Lin Pao turned away. Chou was always so

ridiculously optimistic. At times, it got on his nerves. He straightened his old uniform jacket. It was his only link with the past. He was still very proud to have been an officer in the Chinese People's Navy. The jacket reminded people of that.

'Shouldn't you be going?' Chou suggested, and added quite unnecessarily, 'She doesn't like being kept waiting, does she?'

He met Duang at the bottom of the hundred steps that led to the Dragon Lady's house. The house was the nerve centre of the community. A powerful generator ran night and day to provide the electric power for the pirates' communication links. It was also an Aladdin's cave of valuable booty awaiting sale in Hong Kong or mainland China.

The Dragon Lady was a legend in her own lifetime. Two years ago, Duang had told Lin Pao some of the stories about her, while the rain lashed down and no one could see further than the end of the jetty.

'Her father-in-law fought the Japanese during the Second World War,' Duang had told him. 'Running guns and supplies for the Allies. After the war, they gave him a medal. But he soon got bored with civilian life and went back to his old ways. Couple of years later the Dutch put a price on his head. He was a wanted man again!'

Duang laughed. 'The Dutch still ran Sumatra in those days. They would have hanged him if they'd ever caught him. He had a son. His spitting image. Went out with the boats even as a kid. Learnt all the tricks. Then he met and fell in love with the daughter of a Chinese Triad family. That's her,' Duang had said, jerking his thumb towards the hill. 'The Dragon Lady.

'They made a fantastic team. She could handle a boat as well as any man. She could fight too. Crack shot with a pistol. And she had a head for business which he didn't.'

'Was it her who used to hang pieces of bleeding meat around sailors' necks? To bring in the sharks?' Lin Pao had asked.

'That was her old man. Between you and me, he was a bit of a sadist. She preferred knee-capping.' Duang chuckled. 'Then they got shot up by a British navy patrol. She escaped and spent two days in the water. Some fishermen found her and pulled her out. I heard it was them who told her about this place.'

'Quite a woman,' mused Lin Pao.

'You'd better believe it,' said Duang warmly. 'She's done it all.'

'And this name, the "Dragon Lady", is that her Triad family name or just a nickname someone gave her?'

Duang had looked around then leant across the table. His voice was hoarse. 'The Dragons are Chinese Triads. They've been in Malaysia for years. Very powerful. They're into all sorts of other stuff, if you know what I mean.'

Now, Lin Pao remembered this conversation as he started to climb the hill. In his heart of hearts he was afraid of the Dragon Lady. Not just because she had the power of life or death over him. Lin Pao had lived with violence and sudden death for years. It was a thing one became used to. A part of everyday life.

No! Put simply, she made him feel like a child. And a child in the days when parents held all the cards. He found himself wanting to please her. He needed to win her praise. But he had never discovered how to and it was beginning to obsess him. And now, in a few minutes' time, he was going to have to tell her about last night's near disaster.

'Almost there!' Duang panted.

His words made Lin Pao feel even more depressed. Duang was so utterly predictable. Like a trained dog. He always said, 'Almost there!' at the seventy-seventh step. Lin Pao used to silently count them. Now he no longer bothered. He looked down at the village and saw the tide coming in. A thin line of brown foam was flooding over the mud. He visualized the countless numbers of small crabs racing ahead of it. Crabs intrigued Lin Pao. There were millions of them, all struggling to survive. Each one apparently a clone of its neighbour. Yet in reality, they all lived entirely separate lives. Loners, like himself.

The two men waited on the open veranda, breathing hard and listening for the tap-tapping of her cane. When she appeared, Lin Pao bowed his head. Duang seemed uncomfortable and stood awkwardly.

The Dragon Lady looked very old. Years at sea and the Sumatran climate had seamed her face into a thousand fine lines. Her hair was faded and pulled back in a tight bun. She had lost most of her teeth but her back was ramrod straight. Her eyes were black and shrewd and missed nothing. She was wearing a scarlet brocade jacket, fastened high at the neck.

They all sat down on comfortable bamboo chairs while Nancy, the old lady's maid, poured tea into delicate porcelain bowls. Lin Pao did not like Nancy. She showed him scant respect. She deliberately turned her back on him whenever they met in the village and he was sure she was influencing the boy Duc To, for the worse.

'We will begin with the captains' reports,' the Dragon Lady announced. She rapped her stick on the polished wooden floor and Nancy reappeared to take away the tray.

It was Duang's turn to speak first. His boat had developed engine problems and he had returned early.

'What sort of engine problems?' she demanded. 'Mechanical, electrical or a fuel blockage?'

Duang gulped. 'It could be water leaking into the fuel tank. It happened once before.'

'Then it must not happen again,' she snapped. 'Once is perhaps admissible. Twice is inexcusable. You must take more interest in your boat, Duang. I have told you that before. There are other men who would jump at the chance to be a captain.'

Duang oozed sweat and said nothing.

She turned to Lin Pao. 'I hear you nearly lost everything last night!'

Lin Pao felt his cheeks grow hot. The naughty child again. He made his report as simply and as factually as he could.

'You were lucky!' she told him when he had finished. 'Or that old rogue Sam is a better shot than he ever used to be. Let's hope the Navy boat is not a sign of things to come. You will give Sam a reward of some sort, won't you, Lin Pao? After all, he did save your lives.'

Lin Pao bowed his head.

'Now,' she said briskly. 'We have a visitor to welcome. He will be with us shortly. You both know who he is.'

Duang and Lin Pao had seen the man arrive earlier. He was the Dragon Lady's direct contact with the Family ashore. He was officially known as the 'Courier'.

'Our friends on the mainland have struck gold,' she was telling them. 'There is a ship carrying an extremely valuable cargo coming this way.' She looked meaningfully at both men. 'And your job tonight is to capture her!'

Chapter 10

'Halfway there, Tom,' said Captain Lee, reaching for another sandwich. 'This time tomorrow we'll be docking in Penang. And your mother will be there to meet us.'

Tom frowned. 'Dad! When are you going to get some proper sleep? You've been here on the bridge ever since we left Singapore. And that was ages ago!'

Captain Lee stretched his arms wide and yawned. 'You're right! You're dead right, Tom! But getting through the Straits is the toughest part of the whole voyage.' He slumped back in his chair. 'You've seen how busy it gets? Well, another thirty hours and we'll be finished with the Straits and out into the deep, blue ocean.'

'And I'll be back home,' said Tom morosely.

Tomorrow was his last full day on board. The day

after, the ship had containers to offload at Penang, before she left for Europe.

His father brushed crumbs from his trousers. 'Cheer up! In a couple of years time, you'll just wish you had a shore job. Eight hours' sleep a night in your own bed.' He looked at the helmsman. 'Isn't that right, Wong? Don't you wish you'd stayed on land?'

The man shook his head. 'No, Captain! Not me! I like the sea. No nosy family. No neighbours!' And he laughed.

The *Serota Star* ploughed her way through a darkening sea. The sun had only just set but the horizon was already starting to close in. Tom looked out at the waves and felt his eyes grow hot. It was going to be goodbye to all this. The sound of the ship. The hum of machinery. The soft scrunch of waves under the bow. The friendship of the crew.

He had not anticipated just how different life would be at sea. He was surprised how quickly he had adapted to this new experience. His entire world was now contained within the confines of this ship. His school friends, his activities, even his own mother seemed somehow less important out here. Less real. The crew on board and the ship's progress now filled all his waking thoughts. He wondered if this was how his father felt? And decided, he must.

Captain Lee, meanwhile, had crossed to the back of the bridge and the chart table. 'Come over here, Tom,' he called. 'Show me where we are and what we should be looking out for.'

Together, they pored over the chart. 'There's another lighthouse coming up.' Tom indicated. 'It's called the "Brothers Light". And it flashes every twelve seconds.'

'Good.' His father nodded. 'There's a bad bit to the north-west of it. It's called "Fair Channel Bank". Silly name, considering. Found it?'

Tom had. He peered closely at the chart. 'What do these funny markings mean? They look like fingers spreading out across the channel.'

'Huge underwater sand dunes,' his father told him. 'Ten metres high. Sometimes a lot more. They change shape the whole time depending on the tides and the sea state. It can get pretty rough around there.'

'So if we get too close?'

'We'd go aground in a big way. There's scores of wrecks there. Now,' Captain Lee told him, 'look at the chart again. See the course I've pencilled in to take us clear? Work out how long it'll be before we get there.'

The telephone rang in the bridge console. The officer of the watch listened intently. 'It's the chief engineer,' he said. 'The main bearing's running hot.'

Captain Lee took the telephone. 'Yes, Chief?' he said calmly. 'How bad?' He listened. 'Reckon it'll last until Penang? We've got six hours there. Can you fix it then?' He made a face. 'I don't want to come down in speed. It's rather busy up here. You can? Good!'

'What's happened?' Tom asked the officer of the watch.

'Propellor shaft problems.'

Captain Lee replaced the handset. 'Another long night ahead. Who'd be a sailor?' he asked the bridge at large.

A mile behind them, the navigation lights of a Chinese bulk ore carrier gleamed brightly.

Chapter 11

The Courier was a short plump man who smelt strongly of sandalwood aftershave. He dabbed at his forehead with a spotted red handkerchief. Lin Pao had never known anyone who perspired so much. He stared at the man, trying to make him out. He decided reluctantly that as he held senior rank in the Family, there must be more to him than met the eye.

'Tonight's attack is going to be a little different from what you're used to,' the Courier told them. His voice was surprisingly brisk. He paused to let his words sink in.

'How do you mean, "different"?' Duang asked, belligerently.

The Courier smiled. He was enjoying the moment to the full. It was exciting to have power over these tough, hard men. He paused.

'He's got some high-tech gadgets to make your job easier,' the Dragon Lady told them, bluntly. She was getting bored with the Courier. Why couldn't he just get on with it? There was so much to do to get the boats ready.

The Courier gave her a pained glance. 'Our people in Singapore have fitted some very effective tracking devices to your target ship. No one on board her has any idea they're there. I'm now going to give you the equipment you'll need to find her at sea.'

He stooped and lifted what looked like a laptop on to the table in front of him. He snapped open the locks and beckoned the men to come closer. Lin Pao studied the dials and noted the radio antenna.

'Is it some sort of computer?' asked Duang.

Lin Pao hesitated. 'It picks up signals from the ship?'

The Courier nodded. 'Exactly that! The devices on board beam out a continuous radio signal. This machine's job is to intercept them. All you do then, is to home in on the signal. Well done, Captain.'

He looked across at the Dragon Lady. 'It's the latest and most sophisticated RDF on the market. A Radio Direction Finder, to give it its correct name.'

Duang scowled.

'Don't worry, Duang,' the Dragon Lady called. 'Lin

Pao will be using it. Not you!'

The Courier was enthusing. 'The devices on board the ship are fully activated and on the same frequency as this receiver. See here!' He pointed to a large dial. 'Read out the frequency it's tuned to, will you, Captain?'

'Eighty-eight point one,' Lin Pao told him.

The Courier nodded. 'It's been preset and locked on to that frequency. You've just got to plug it in to your existing on-board system and switch on when you're at sea. Don't worry,' he added. 'We'll have a practice run-through before I leave.'

'What sort of range has it got?' asked the Dragon Lady.

'Anything up to fifty kilometres. But in your case, a small boat low in the water, I'd say not more than fifteen.'

'Show them what else you've brought.'

Like a conjuror, the Courier rummaged in his bag and produced two small packages. 'Infrared torches to communicate with. And goggles to see the flashes. You'll be able to know where each of you is even on the darkest night.'

'That's good,' Lin Pao said. 'My radar is still not working.'

'You'd better practise with them as soon as it gets dark,' the Dragon Lady told them. 'And Lin Pao! You'll need to work out a simple code for using them.'

'We've never needed to use these things before, so why now?' grumbled Duang.

The Dragon Lady clicked her tongue. 'Duang! You great ox! We need them because we've never played for stakes this high before. That's why!'

'Just how high are they?' Lin Pao asked.

The Dragon Lady looked at the Courier.

'About twenty million American dollars,' he said, quietly.

Lin Pao's mouth dropped open.

'And that information is not to go outside this room,' the Dragon Lady snapped. 'Do you both understand? I don't want the crews to know in case they get overexcited. This has to go to plan. If it doesn't, I'll know who to blame!'

There was an uncomfortable silence.

'When do we sail?' Duang asked.

'Tonight. At dusk,' she said. 'We've not got long. So let's make the plan. And make it a good one!'

Chapter 12

'All this radio finding stuff sounds great in theory,' grumbled Duang, as they walked along the jetty towards their boats, 'but I bet it won't be quite as easy at midnight in a gale in the middle of the Straits.'

That was true of course but Lin Pao could have done without it. Duang's role in the operation was quite small, while he had the entire responsibility of finding this *Serota Star* ship.

The Family had worked out where the ship should be and by when. Additionally, the shipping lane she had to use was comparatively narrow, a mere twelve miles across. But, and he knew only too well that it was a very big, 'But', so much depended on chance. A hundred things could go wrong. Sudden squalls, freak waves, engine failure, naval patrols . . . Lin Pao could imagine them all. Whatever happened, unexpected or not, they'd blame him. The Family might even kill him. He was expendable. They all were, except for the Dragon Lady.

The crews watched their captains climb on board. No one said anything. The pirates were puzzled. And becoming restless. Something out of the ordinary was happening and they had not been told what. No one fired off a volley of gunfire. There were no whoops or cheers. And their families had gathered in silence on the jetty, looking uncertain.

The men at the heavy machine guns in the bows swung them in an arc across the sky in a forlorn attempt to impress the onlookers. Then they looked around sheepishly and pretended to be interested in something else. The boats' engines fired and clouds of exhaust gathered at their sterns.

'Cast off!' Lin Pao ordered. He shot a quick glance towards the big house on the hill. For a second he clearly saw the Dragon Lady standing there and the child Nancy, to one side of her. He thought she raised her stick in farewell but by then the bows of the *Ular Ular* were swinging round in the tide.

Chou, the bosun, looked across at him. 'Skipper?' he prompted.

Lin Pao nodded and concentrated on taking them to

sea. The beat of the engines deepened and they were out in the middle of the river, heading for the great bend and the deep water under the cliffs. The sound died away and the wash of their passing exhausted itself amongst the fishing traps staked out in the shallows. The watching crowd drifted home.

It was less than a mile to the estuary and almost dark by the time they reached it. Beyond the mangroves, they could hear the boom of the surf. Duang brought his boat alongside Lin Pao. This was where the pirates did their final checks.

'One hour to wait,' Lin Pao told him.

Duang nodded and slapped at a mosquito. The mangroves were home to millions of the insects which bit with a savagery that even the pirates could not ignore for long. A man would suddenly break into a frenzy of curses, goaded beyond reason. This was when tempers ran high, threats were exchanged and scuffles broke out. So they chain-smoked, partly to keep the mosquitoes at bay and partly to relieve the boredom.

'We've got to tell them something,' Duang said. 'Or they'll get nasty.'

Lin Pao shook his head. 'She told us not to say anything,' he reminded Duang. 'Give them an extra shot of rum. They'll be happy with that.'

Later, they went through the details of the attack again and the hijacking of the ship. Duang wrote the radio code words they would use in thick grease pencil on the inside of the bridge windscreen. Finally, both men checked their watches and nodded to one another. The engine note of Duang's craft swelled and it was gone. A lean shadow slipping unseen into the night.

Lin Pao put on his infrared goggles. Taking careful aim, he flashed the torch into the darkness. With an immense feeling of relief, he counted four flashes in reply. Flashes that were invisible to the naked eye.

Lin Pao grinned. It might even be an omen. The thought cheered him. Chou looked at him speculatively but said nothing. The moon was just cutting the horizon when Lin Pao took *Ular Ular* out into the open sea. When they were clear of the shoals, he swung the wheel over and headed south to intercept the expected track of the *Serota Star*.

Chapter 13

Later that evening, Sergeant Chung parked his car outside his wife's office and went in to collect her. The night-watchman was sitting behind a desk in the cramped reception area. A pile of out-of-date magazines lay scattered across a low table.

Sergeant Chung walked down an airless corridor to her office.

'You've had a long day,' he observed.

Mrs Chung yawned. 'I've been having a problem with one of my suppliers,' she said. 'Silly man. I won't be using him again.'

'Ready to go?' he prompted.

She nodded and began tidying her desk. 'Nice boy, that Tom Lee. He'll be the spitting image of his father when he's older.' She gave a final glance at some papers then remembered something.

'Could you switch off the photocopier in the back, please? Oh! And make sure I've left nothing important there. Do you mind?'

'Sure.' He walked through into the next room. He lifted the top of the copier and, as he did so, a piece of paper slipped out. He made a grab for it and missed. The paper slid down behind the machine.

He peered over the top. He could see it but couldn't quite get his hand down between the copier and the fax machine that stood beside it. Carefully, he eased the copier out from the wall and leant over to retrieve the page. As he did so, he saw something he was not expecting. His eyes saw it but because he was also tired, its significance did not register.

But five minutes later, he gave an exclamation and pulled off the motorway.

'What's the matter?' demanded Mrs Chung. 'What are you doing?'

'I'm sorry,' he said. 'There's something I must check.'

'Check what?' She sounded irritable.

'Something in your office.'

By this time, they were heading back the way they had come. A couple of minutes later, a very cross Mrs Chung was fitting her office key into the lock.

'You're mad!' she cried as he pushed past her. 'You've

been watching too many late night detective films!'

But Sergeant Chung was too busy to reply. He pulled the fax machine out from the wall and knelt down beside it. He gave a whistle of triumph.

'What have you found?'

Silently, he pointed to the thick plastic collar wrapped around the mains cable and the thin, black wire that disappeared into the wall.

Mrs Chung stared at him. 'What is it?'

'It's a tap. A bug. That's what!'

'A bug? You mean . . .'

'I'm no expert,' he interrupted. 'But at a guess I'd say someone else is very keen to know what's in the faxes you send and receive.'

Mrs Chung looked horror-stricken. 'But they're in code,' she gasped.

Sergeant Chung stood up straight and looked at her.

'Judging by the sophistication of this little item, I don't think the average commercial code would stay a mystery for long with these people. I think we've got trouble. Big trouble.'

Chapter 14

Midnight! And still no sign of the *Serota Star*. Lin Pao drummed his fingers against the side of the bridge. And waited. There was nothing else to do. For the past five hours, the *Ular Ular* had zigzagged across the shipping lane searching for her target. And in all that time, the RDF equipment had remained silent. Its solitary red light glowing unwaveringly in the dark.

Twenty other ships had lumbered by in that time and with each one that sailed past, the crew had become more restless. In the end, Chou had been forced to hit one of them with the length of lead piping he always carried when they were at sea. Ever since then, the crew had lain slouched across the deck, complaining to one another in low voices.

So now they waited at the southern end of a small island, their engine just turning over. Duang's boat was keeping station three hundred metres behind. Occasionally, Duang would flash them meaningless infrared signals. Whether he was doing this by accident or on purpose, Lin Pao could not decide. But all it did was to add to his own growing sense of panic. His brain seethed with worries and the possibilities of what might have gone wrong.

Perhaps the *Serota Star* had already sailed past, before the pirates had arrived? Lin Pao's blood ran cold at the thought. Perhaps there was something wrong with the RDF receiver. Or, worse, there was something he had forgotten to do! What if the *Serota Star* had broken down or even been attacked by another crew! The one thing no one had thought about was the possibility of her being attacked by other pirates! He peered at his watch. It was time to resume patrolling.

'Have some tea,' said Chou, coming up from the galley. Lin Pao took it gratefully. Despite the oppressive heat, he was shivering. His feet were icy cold. That was the trouble with being a perfectionist. Nerves!

'There's bad weather coming,' Chou told him.

Lin Pao looked up. Chou was right. The moon had disappeared some time ago and now the sky was covered with a great blanket of cloud. The wind was rising.

Chou wiped a ragged sleeve across his brow.

'Tide's turned,' he said conversationally. 'Sea's getting up.' He pointed into the darkness beyond the bows, where successive waves were bursting on a reef. The *Ular Ular*'s engine was turning just enough to counter the suck of the waves towards it.

'This machine of yours,' he asked, jerking a thumb at the RDF receiver. 'Reliable, is it?'

'God alone knows,' Lin Pao replied bitterly.

Chou considered. 'And we're supposed to keep this up till dawn?'

'Could be longer.'

Chou swore and was about to say something, when the sudden crackle of radio static filled the bridge. Red and green lights began to flash on the receiver. Lin Pao stared at it in disbelief.

'It's working now!' Chou exclaimed. 'The damn thing's working all right!'

Lin Pao stood riveted, listening to a high-pitched signal like a hungry mosquito grow louder. There was no mistake about it. The target had arrived! The crew crowded in to look, their sullenness miraculously gone. There were smiles and puzzled laughter all around.

'OK! OK! You've all seen it,' shouted Chou. 'Now get out there and start looking. Big reward for the first man to spot her!'

The *Ular Ular* throbbed with new purpose. Lin Pao waited until he saw Duang's answering torch flashes then brought his boat round in a great sweeping turn. The radio signal wavered. Lin Pao juggled with the wheel, searching for the right direction to follow. A wave burst over the bow, soaking the crew, who yelled in excitement. The radio signal grew stronger and Lin Pao knew that, at last, the *Serota Star* lay directly ahead of them.

The bridge of the *Serota Star* was bathed in purple night light. The young officer of the watch was checking the radar. He noticed the two small blips that had not been there before. He wondered where they had come from and decided they must have been behind the nearby island. Almost certainly fishing boats.

He concentrated instead on the bigger ships around them. The Straits were beginning to open out, with deeper water on either side of them. This was where ship's captains would want to put as much distance as possible between one another. They would also start cracking on speed. The officer also noticed the storm racing down on all of them.

He looked across at Captain Lee. The man was slumped in his chair, fast asleep. His head was resting on the bridge window.

'I'm just going to take a quick look outside,' he told the helmsman, and stepped out on to the bridge wing.

The helmsman nodded then returned to the humdrum of his own thoughts.

'Get ready!' Lin Pao shouted as the *Serota Star*'s stern loomed above them. He glanced along the ship's side, using a line of brightly lit portholes as a marker. Just in front of them, the rumble and splash of the propeller warned of the danger they were in. One mistake and the *Ular Ular* would be matchwood.

He caught the sudden smell of warm earth and the next moment, the wind came howling down. Rain cascaded over them, blotting out everything. The *Ular Ular* shuddered. For one terrible moment, Lin Pao thought they had been thrust into the propeller.

'We're too close! Too close!' Chou screamed in his ear.

Lin Pao fought for control while the *Ular Ular* bucked and twisted like a maddened bull. He guessed they were not more than ten metres from the cliff-like hull. It was impossible to see. His head was hunched down into his shoulders, both eyes almost closed as the rain streamed down his face. He had no idea where Chou was, or what he was doing. The two vessels seemed tied together, pitching and swooping on parallel tracks.

Then, as suddenly as it had come, the wind dropped and with it the rain. Lin Pao cut their speed and watched the great hull slide past. For a moment, his legs threatened to buckle. Chou clapped a hand on his shoulder. The next moment, he was back out on deck, shouting at the crew and kicking them into position.

Lin Pao brought them in again. He saw the grappling-hooks swinging.

'Throw!'

The hooks went flying up and caught.

'Now, CLIMB! CLIMB! Get up there!' Lin Pao screamed and scrambled after them.

Tom opened his eyes. Something had woken him. He stretched out an arm and switched on the light above his bunk. He sat up and looked around the cabin. Someone was running along the corridor outside. Not one person, several. Why were they shouting?

Tom threw off his sheet and scrambled up. As he tugged on his shorts, the door burst open. A strange, dishevelled-looking man stood there, glaring at him. He was soaked to the skin and panting hard. There was a long curved knife in his right hand.

He screamed something at Tom and came towards him. Tom put his fists up. Another man came bursting in, grabbed Tom's arm and twisted it high up behind his back. The boy cried out in pain as they bundled him along the corridor. They wrenched back the sliding door at the far end with a bang and pushed Tom on to the bridge.

The bridge was full of the same violent men. Pirates! What else could they be! Two of them carried rifles. The rest all seemed to have knives or pangas in their hands. 'Dad!' he shouted. Captain Lee was sprawled on the deck by the chart table, nursing his head. One of the pirates bent over and hauled him to his feet.

'Dad!' yelled Tom. 'Dad! You all right?'

Someone shouted at him. A man in some sort of uniform jacket. Tom ignored him.

'Take it easy, Tom! These men mean business!'

An arm came from behind and locked across Tom's throat, cutting off his breath. He kicked backwards with his heel and stamped down as hard as he could on the man's foot. There was a loud yell in his ear and the suffocating grip loosened. He spun around, ducking and fending off his assailant with all the strength he could muster. The pirate slipped in a pool of water and went down. His knife clattered on to the deck.

Tom reached for it but even as he touched the handle, a blow caught him on the side of the head. He went sprawling. Strong hands pulled him back to his feet. Someone slapped him across the face. It was like being hit with a brick. There was blood in his mouth. A lot of it. His teeth felt loose.

'Who is this boy?' Lin Pao demanded, his fist twisting into Captain Lee's hair, dragging his head back.

'My son!' he gasped.

Lin Pao stared at Tom.

'Good!' he said. 'Now we'll have a hostage to make sure you cooperate.'

There was a burst of shouting from the bridge wing. Duang and two of his men appeared.

'We've done it! We've done it!' Duang cried, punching the air in elation. He grinned at Lin Pao. 'We've rounded them all up. They're waiting like mice.'

'Excellent!' Lin Pao said and allowed himself a rare grin. He turned to Chou. 'Get a searchlight on them. And bring the captain and his brat with you. I want them all to see what happens next.'

Down on the main deck, two more pirates with AK47 rifles stood guard over the *Serota Star*'s crew. The steel deck glinted in the sudden blaze of light. The crew were squatting on their haunches, their hands on top of their heads. Some of them were crying. Others were pleading with their guards. The hair rose at the back of Tom's neck. A pirate pushed him down beside his father.

Lin Pao climbed up on to a hatch and stood gazing down at them. Robert, the steward who had looked after Tom, began to scream. Lin Pao pointed to him. Robert became hysterical and started to throw himself from side to side.

'That one!' Lin Pao commanded.

Duang and another pirate grabbed Robert by the collar and began to drag him towards the ship's side.

'This is what will happen to any of you who disobey orders,' Lin Pao shouted.

Duang lifted him up above the rail and with a quick heave pitched the man overboard. There was a scream, a faint splash . . . then silence.

Captain Lee was on his feet, shouting and struggling. Lin Pao jumped down and pointed a revolver at his head.

'You have a job to do for us, Captain,' he cried. 'If you do it well, your son will live. If you do not, the boy will join the sharks. Now which is it to be?'

Chapter 15

Tom was helpless. And in pain. His hands and feet had been expertly tied together. There was no give of any sort and the rope was cutting into his skin. He lay on his side unable to stop himself sliding over the cold, wet deck whenever the boat rolled heavily. His head ached, his face was sore and his right arm felt as if it had been wrenched out of its socket. But worst of all, he was thirsty. Desperately thirsty.

He raised his head and saw the sky was turning grey. Dawn was coming. The start of a day he didn't want to know anything about. And that brought the terror of the night rushing back. Where was his father? What was happening to him? When would he see him again? And poor old Robert! Had these evil, wicked men really thrown him overboard? Or was that all a dream?

Three metres away, he could see a man's bare feet, balancing as the boat heaved and swooped through the waves. Tom could hear him singing. Singing! Without a care in the world.

Anger flared inside him. Who gave these men, these criminals, the right to do this? He tried to struggle up but failed. Spray came over the side of the boat and spattered his face. He licked his lips and tasted salt. His mouth was as dry as sand. He must have water.

'Water! I need water!' He tried to shout but it came out instead as a dry croaking.

He saw the man's feet turn then come towards him. He flinched, waiting for a kick. Instead, the man grabbed him by his T-shirt and sat him upright. He reached over towards a side locker.

'Here!' said Chou. 'Have this!' He bent over Tom and held a bottle to the boy's mouth.

Tom sucked greedily while water ran down over his chest. He couldn't get enough of it. It was the most wonderful sensation he had known. His eyes closed. Eventually, he turned his head away. 'Thanks!' he said, speaking as gruffly as he could.

Chou sat back on his haunches and looked at him. 'So you're the tough guy, eh?' And he laughed. 'Chancing it a bit, weren't you? Attacking Ho like that!

Got a nasty temper, Ho has. I'd keep clear of him if I was you.'

'What do you mean "attack"? When you go round murdering people! Come off it!'

Chou stood up and looked around, checking the sea in front of them. By now, it was full daylight. Last night's cloud cover had disappeared and the sky was pink along the horizon with the promise of a fine day to come. He sat on the bridge chair, half facing the boy.

'Ho would have cut you to ribbons. You were lucky.' He looked past Tom then raised an arm over his head and began to wave.

With an effort, Tom pushed himself up higher and twisted round to see. There was another pirate boat not much more than two hundred metres behind. A large wave rolled under *Ular Ular* and Tom fell over. Chou made no attempt to help him up.

'Well,' he said, watching Tom's efforts with interest, 'I'll give you one thing. You were the only one who put up a fight. Stupid thing to do, mind!'

'So what's happening now?' Tom demanded. 'Where's my dad?'

'He'll be all right,' Chou answered. 'So long as he does what he's told.'

'But where is he? What's he doing?'

Anxiety welled up inside him. He thought of his father alone on the bridge. Surrounded by people like Ho, waiting for the word to put a knife in his ribs. Tom's eyes were suddenly very hot. But there was no way he was going to cry in front of this man! No way!

Chou cupped his hands and lit a cigarette. He hesitated then came over to the boy and offered it to him.

Tom almost burst into tears there and then. The man was actually being kind. He was almost human!

'What are they making my dad do?' he asked after a long pause.

'He's bringing the ship in,' and seeing Tom's puzzled face, added, 'for a repaint. And a name change.'

Tom considered this. 'Then what?'

'Then he takes her back out. Somewhere in China. Canton, possibly. Or some little port along the coast. Not that it's any business of yours.' He studied Tom thoughtfully. 'You're a nosy little so-and-so, aren't you?'

'What about me? Am I going with him?'

Chou laughed. The idea genuinely amused him. 'You go with him? Of course not! You're a hostage. If your father does the business, you'll be OK.'

'And if he doesn't?' Tom asked.

Chou chuckled. 'Let's just say we're all expecting him to do well.'

A silence fell.

'So what'll I be doing?' Tom persisted, after a moment.

'There's lots of jobs for a boy like you. Helping in the cookhouse, for starters. Or you can keep the boats clean. Lots of things.' Chou took a long drag on his cigarette then flicked it over the side. 'And if you'd like to join us,' he went on, 'then keep your nose clean for a couple of years and maybe we'll let you!' He stood up and began waving to the boat behind.

'Please!' called Tom. 'Untie me? Only I can't feel my hands or feet. There's no circulation.'

To his surprise, Chou seized him by the shoulders, lifted him straight up, carried him over and dumped him down in the captain's chair. He stabbed a finger into the boy's face. 'You just sit tight. Got it? We're almost there. Don't touch nothing. If you do, I'll break your arms. Understand?'

Tom nodded. Chou was a frighteningly strong man. He took a deep breath and looked around. He was surprised to see how close they were to land. At a guess, they were less than a mile off shore. The sea was discoloured with mud so they must be near the mouth of a river. There were reefs on either side of them but some distance away. Tom could see waves breaking over them. They were following a wide channel towards a line of mangrove swamps. There were hills behind them, covered in jungle.

Chou took the *Ular Ular* straight on past the mangroves. The boat's wake ruffled the chocolate-coloured water. Not far ahead, the river ran between cliffs where the throb of the *Ular*'s engine beat back loudly, from the rock walls. Families of monkeys crashed through the treetops, keeping pace with them.

'Can you really get my father's ship in here?' Tom asked.

'It's deep enough. Used to be an old volcano or something. It'll be tight turning her around but we've done it before.' Then Chou added, 'I thought I told you to shut up!'

Tom could hardly believe it. Were the pirates really going to bring the *Serota Star* along here? Why? Then he remembered what the man had told him. A 'repaint'. So how many people would that take to do?

There was a bend ahead of them. A long bend that seemed to go on for ever. Tom thought it must be at least a mile long. An awful thought struck him. What happened if the *Serota Star* did get stuck after all? What would happen then? Would they blame his father? He blew out his cheeks in worry. It got no easier.

Chou was humming again and clearly in high spirits. Several times he looked across at Tom as if he was going to say something but thought better of it. Then, he flung out an arm and said, 'Watch!'

The river spread out dramatically. It now formed a wide bowl, partly surrounded by tall cliffs. A natural harbour. The ground on the left bank, however, was much lower and had sunk down to river level. On this side, the jungle gave way to clumps of flowering plants and bushes. There were mango and breadfruit trees and stands of tall palms.

And amongst them, Tom saw the huts. A dozen at least. There were more, further back in the trees, and still others coming into view, perched on stilts, high above the river. Small wooden boats were drawn up along the shore. Fishing nets were draped over poles. A long, wooden landing-stage jutted out into the river. And there were people everywhere!

Tom could see children. They came running, waving at the boat and calling excitedly. The little ones were naked. The bigger boys came splashing through the shallows and diving in towards them. There were women gathering like humming-birds and flocking on to the landing-stage. It was beautiful and the last thing Tom had been expecting.

A klaxon horn blared beside him. Chou cut the engines. The *Ular Ular* drifted towards the jetty. There was a gentle bump.

'How do you like your new home?' Chou asked with a grin.

Chapter 16

Sergeant Chung studied the building carefully. It had once been a prosperous factory employing two hundred people or more. Now its tin roof was rusted and sagging and its windows were jagged with broken glass. Weeds grew waist high on either side of the barbed wire fence that ran beside the road. It was one of a number of similar places along here, long ago abandoned and now strewn with rubbish.

It was also the operational headquarters of a small but highly effective electronic monitoring unit, run by the Singapore Police's 'Organized Crime Division'. Visitors were not encouraged. Not many police officers even knew of its existence. The men and women who worked here spent their lives listening in to the murky and dangerous world of serious crime. The building they operated from was totally in character.

The early morning sun was warm on his back as Sergeant Chung picked his way between the potholes. He was dressed as a labourer. No one else would be walking through this industrial wasteland so early in the day.

Casually, he plodded towards the old main gate. There was a bell push at shoulder height. He pressed it. Two short rings and a long one. The prearranged signal. He waited with drooping shoulders, while his eyes searched for the concealed CCTV camera. It took a while before he spotted it, high up in a broken streetlight. There was a quiet buzz beside him and the gate clicked open. He pushed through and heard it slam shut.

'Go down the left-hand side till you come to a red door. That's your way in. We'll meet you there,' they had told him.

He found the door without any problem. Two men were waiting for him inside.

'Your ID card,' said the shorter one, holding out his hand. He turned his back on Sergeant Chung and spoke quietly into a microphone.

'OK,' he said, looking up moments later. 'Follow me.' There were no further introductions.

Friendly lot, thought Sergeant Chung.

As they walked in silence through the building, Sergeant Chung shook his head in admiration. The place was a wonderful piece of deception. New ceilings had been installed. Strip lights hummed overhead. There were rooms full of equipment and banks of computers. In front of them, people with headphones sat absorbed.

They stepped through another door and out into daylight again. They were in a closed inner courtyard that had once housed the loading bays. On the far side, a heavy steel door blocked all access to the outside world.

A nondescript van was waiting. Sergeant Chung knew it was for them. The van had a battered look to it. There were numerous scratches and dents along its sides. The name of a previous owner could just be made out beneath a later coat of paint. The rear windows were covered with masking tape.

The taller man pulled open the back doors. 'This is the best-equipped van we have,' he said.

Sergeant Chung nodded his thanks.

'You're lucky it's available,' the man sniffed.

The shorter man jerked a thumb towards the rear doors. 'You'll be in there with him.'

Sergeant Chung peered inside. There were two

uncomfortable-looking stools bolted to the floor. Neither had a back rest. In front of them, there was a long map table hinged to the driver's side of the van. Someone had already pinned a street map in place. The rest of the space was crammed with aerials and computers. At the far end, a large TV-like screen ran the width of the vehicle. There was a gun rack just inside the back door. It held two shotguns.

'Not much room,' Sergeant Chung said and wished he hadn't. It didn't sound very professional. 'How accurate can you be?' he went on quickly.

'Tell him!' the shorter man ordered.

His companion shrugged. 'We can hear a fly burp,' he told Sergeant Chung. 'We get within a few metres of a source.' He grinned suddenly. 'That little bug in your wife's office. I had a look at it last night. It's got an operating range of a couple of hundred metres. So it's only a matter of time before we find where its parent is.'

'And then it's up to me.'

'It's not quite so easy,' the smaller man warned. 'There're a lot of buildings all squashed together down there by the docks. So there's going to be a lot of screening. Could take all day. Easy!'

Sergeant Chung looked relieved. 'Well that doesn't sound bad to me.'

They gave him a sour grin.

'I forgot to tell you,' the bigger man said. 'There's no air-conditioning. And once we're inside, we stay put.'

'Otherwise you'll blow our cover,' his companion warned. 'You'll probably feel different in a couple of hours!' He looked at his watch. 'It's seven o'clock now. If we get nothing by midday, we'll come back here for a pit stop. OK! Let's go!'

Sergeant Chung clambered inside. The doors banged shut. Moments later, the engine started. He squirmed on his seat. It was like sitting on concrete. He turned to make a comment but the tall man had his earphones on. He was engrossed in checking his equipment, flicking switches here, checking dials there. He was in his own little world.

Sergeant Chung took a deep breath. It was going to be a long, long day and the words 'pit stop' were already taking on an urgency all of their own.

Chapter 17

'It's a big ship!' exclaimed Nancy.

Duc To gave a whistle. 'I never thought they'd turn her around!' He shook his head in amazement. 'That was really something!'

The roar of the anchor chain sounded across the water and the *Serota Star* lay quietly at her moorings. She filled the river in front of them. On the far side, her stern was almost touching the cliffs. Over here, her bow was less than two hundred metres from the landing-stage. The watching crowd gasped and gave a ragged cheer. The pirates lining her side waved and the cheering grew louder.

Duc To looked puzzled. 'But what's she doing here? What's so special?' He looked at the girl. 'It's the first time I've ever seen them do that. Bring a ship in here.'

'Money! Big money!' Nancy replied, impatiently. 'I

told you. Why don't you ever listen? There's thousands and thousands of PlayStations and iPods on board. All the latest stuff.'

'What happens if an aircraft goes over? They'll see the ship! Then what?'

Nancy looked at him scornfully. 'When did you last see a plane fly over here?'

Duc To considered. 'You're right!' He looked suitably impressed. 'So what are they doing with the ship?'

'Well,' she told him importantly, 'first, they're going to disguise her then they'll give her a new name.'

'How do you mean "disguise her"?'

'They're going to paint her! Stupid! They're sending a boat full of paint here tomorrow morning.'

'Then what?'

Nancy looked quickly over her shoulder. Her voice dropped. 'I heard the Dragon Lady say they were probably sailing her to Canton. She reckons that's where they'll get the best price. All the top people in the Family are coming here tonight for a big meeting,' she confided. 'But you're not to say I told you! Promise?'

Duc To nodded. 'Like always.' He thought for a moment, then, 'Who's the boy Chou brought back?'

'He's the captain's son.' She indicated the *Serota Star*.

'Is he a slave like us?'

Nancy tossed her head. 'Well, yes. But only until they hear the ship's got there safely. Then they'll let him go. Take him across to the mainland.'

Duc To rubbed a foot in the dust. 'You really think they'll do that?'

She frowned. 'I don't know. But I'll find out. I hear everything.' Her face cleared. 'Why don't we go and have a look at him? Then I'd better get her lunch ready. Come on!'

Chapter 18

Tom was also watching the *Serota Star* drop anchor. For the past hour, he had been cleaning out cooking pots at the river's edge. A lump formed in his throat as he saw the ship appear. The *Serota Star* was soon towering over the village. He scrambled to his feet and started to wave his arms high above his head. No one waved back. His eyes scanned the bridge windows, searching for his father. There was no sign of movement behind the tinted glass.

The villagers were crowding on to the jetty, chattering and laughing in delight. Tom had never felt quite so alone before. Surely his father had seen him? Why couldn't he come out on to the bridge wing and give him a quick wave?

He watched the bows of the ship turn slowly towards him. A few minutes later, he was looking directly up at her bridge. This time, he jumped up and down, waving and shouting at the top of his voice. His father must see him. He had to. How could he miss him? They were barely two hundred metres apart.

A heavy kick sent Tom flying head first into the river. He swallowed a mouthful of water the wrong way and came up fighting for breath. He couldn't breathe! He knelt knee deep in the river, for what seemed an eternity, while an enormous iron band started to crush his chest. He had no idea how long he stayed like this. Five seconds? Ten? It felt like eternity before he could breathe properly again. He looked up and saw a squat little man with piggy eyes and a greasy ponytail standing there. It was the cook.

He was screaming at the boy. A tirade of abuse. Tom listened to it and saw the knife at his belt. He felt his own anger subside. What could he do against a man like this? He squelched towards the place where the cooking pots were heaped on the sand.

'You get those done right now!' the cook screamed. 'Or I'll report you!'

Tom wondered whom he'd be reported to. Some other thug, obviously. He didn't bother replying. Instead he squatted down but couldn't help wincing as he did so. The man's foot had caught Tom high up on the leg and it was feeling painful. He scooped up a handful of wet sand and started scouring the top of a container.

The cook, who had seen the boy grimace, smiled sourly. 'You bring them to me in ten minutes,' he shouted. 'Or I'll beat you!' His hand slapped at the thick leather belt he wore around his waist.

'You and whose army?' Tom muttered as he stomped off.

He waited until the man was out of sight then turned to watch his father's ship. He hoped his father hadn't been on the bridge. Captain Lee would have enough on his plate without seeing his son being bullied.

Tom watched both pirate boats go alongside the ship. Rope-ladders were flung over the side of the *Serota Star* and the pirates were soon swarming down. Tom counted fourteen of them. He guessed there would be more left on board to keep an eye on the ship's crew. He wondered where they all were and decided the pirates must have locked them up.

He remembered what Chou had told him. He was a hostage for his father's good behaviour. If all went well, and Captain Lee took the *Serota Star* to where the pirates wanted, they would both be safe. And set free.

He wondered how long that would take. A week? A month? But until then, he was a prisoner.

He stood up and gave a final wave to the ship. Then he bent down and started picking up the pot lids. He remembered his mother putting away the saucepans at home. They had washed up together after supper that last night in Penang. There was a lump in his throat as a wave of homesickness swept over him. And for the first time since this nightmare started, he found himself sobbing.

Chapter 19

It was like an oven inside the van. Three o'clock in the afternoon and the fumes and heat of the city broke in silent waves on the tin box they were sitting in. For the sixth time that minute, Sergeant Chung shifted position on the muscle-numbing hardness of the stool.

He glanced irritably at the tall technician beside him and silently cursed the man for his calm indifference to discomfort. Just like a damn robot, Sergeant Chung thought. Nothing seemed to bother him. His only concern was the job in hand.

His colleague, who was driving, called over his shoulder, 'Turning into Cherry Street.'

Sergeant Chung looked at the map and watched the technician's finger trace their progress. Privately, he was beginning to despair. They had already spent seven hours driving around very slowly and had only covered about half the area around the shipping office. Sergeant Chung didn't think he could take much more of it.

'Perhaps the crooks have switched their device thing off,' he grumbled. 'I mean, it's a possibility, isn't it?'

The tall man looked puzzled. Then his brow cleared and he smiled at Sergeant Chung. It was a superior smile. The smile of one who knows better. He shook his head. 'It doesn't work like that.'

He searched for a Biro and started to draw a diagram on a piece of scrap paper. He spun it round and pushed it towards Sergeant Chung. 'That bug you found in your wife's office. Remember?'

Sergeant Chung gave him a look.

The man didn't seem to notice. 'Well, that bug's job was to intercept all fax traffic coming in and to relay it back, to a third party. And those people are the ones we're calling the "Crooks". Right?'

Sergeant Chung nodded.

'Now, remember there was a little black wire there beside it? The one that led through to that neat little transmitter we found, on the other side of her wall?'

Outside the van, two men had begun quarrelling over a parking space. Sergeant Chung thought their raised voices could have come from aliens in outer space. It was all so . . . what was the word? Surreal. Yes! It was all so surreal.

'Now then,' the tall man was saying. 'That same little transmitter happens to be sending out its own radio signal. It can't help it. And it doesn't matter what else the crooks may have switched off, that little transmitter will just go on broadcasting.' He beamed at Sergeant Chung. 'It's a bit like breathing. It doesn't matter if you're wide awake or fast asleep. You're still breathing. Your lungs are working. Agreed?'

Sergeant Chung thought he understood.

'And that's what I'm listening for!' He waved a hand. 'With all the kit we've got in here, we'll find where these crooks are. Don't you worry. It's only a matter of time.'

Sergeant Chung stared glassy-eyed at the map in front of him. Could he stand two more hours squashed up in this hell-hole? He'd give everything he owned for a cold shower. Or a swim in the sea. And that made him think of Tom Lee. He wondered where the boy had got to? Wasn't it today, they were due to dock in Penang?

'Listen! That's it!' hissed the tall man in excitement. He twisted around to a new monitor, his fingers flying over the switches. There was a sudden mush of electronic noise then a high-pitched whistle that grew louder and deeper, as he fine-tuned the controls. The moment the sound reached the bottom of the scale, he called out, 'Zero beat!'

The van braked to a stop. Sergeant Chung heard the driver's door open then slam shut after him. The tall man meanwhile was ecstatic. He was crooning out loud and rocking back and forth in delight. 'We've got them! We've got them!'

Sergeant Chung grinned. The discomfort and frustration of the long day was already rapidly disappearing. 'What's happening out there? What's he doing? The driver, I mean?'

The tall man nodded happily. 'He's got the bonnet up, pretending to be fixing the engine. Checking the place out.'

The driver came back and flung himself back into his seat. 'Number 112 Cherry Street. It's a funny place! There's a big, green elephant on the stairs right outside the front door. It's a toy factory! Something like that!'

The tall man laughed. 'Well, it's original. I'll give them that.' He turned to Sergeant Chung. 'So what are you going to do about that?'

* * *

Back at his own headquarters, Sergeant Chung went straight to the Commissioner's office. 'We've found the place, sir! A toy factory on Cherry Street. I'd like every bit of information we have on the place and the owner. Who his friends are. Who his clients are. His police and tax record. Where he lives. Everything. Then, I'd like to take a quiet look around.'

'Fine,' said Commissioner. 'I'll set the wheels in motion. You can start on it first thing tomorrow morning.'

But when Sergeant Chung arrived to collect his wife soon afterwards, he found her beside herself with worry.

'It's the *Serota Star*!' she told him. 'She's four hours overdue at Penang and we've not heard a word of her since yesterday. She's not answering her radio.' She put her head in her hands. 'She's just disappeared. But she can't. Can she?'

Sergeant Chung stood stock-still. It had happened. 'Oh my God!' he whispered. Then to cover his own confusion, he strode over and put an arm around her shoulders.

'It's that spare part she had fitted!' he reassured her. 'That was for her radio. Remember? It must have gone again.' He tried to smile. 'She'll be there later tonight. You'll see!'

A little later, he made an excuse and went out to telephone the Commissioner from a secure line. He told him what he wanted to do next.

'Get on with it!' the Commissioner ordered.

Chapter 20

There was a sharp rap on the cabin door. Captain Lee swung his legs off the bunk as the door was unlocked. Lin Pao stood there. With an exclamation, Captain Lee got to his feet. The pirate noted the shaving cut on the other man's chin and the clean white uniform shirt he was wearing.

His eyes flickered. He was secretly amused. Captain Lee was deliberately doing everything he could to keep up his morale and pretend that everything was normal.

'You've had breakfast?' Lin Pao asked, seeing the half-finished tray.

Captain Lee stepped forward. 'I want to see my son! I demand to see my son!' His voice rose. 'Where is he? And why am I a prisoner on my own ship?'

Lin Pao replied, matter of factly, 'You are confined to your cabin. I've already told you.'

Captain Lee suddenly shouted. 'I'm doing nothing until I've seen Tom. D'you hear?'

Lin Pao sighed. Silly man! he thought. What did all this display of anger matter? The man and his son were victims. Their fate was unavoidable. There was nothing either of them could do about it. But outwardly he said, 'Wait here.' And he shouted for Chou, the bosun, who came almost at once.

'The Captain's son,' he told Chou. 'Where is he? And what is he doing?'

Chou scratched his head. 'He's in the cookhouse. Least, that's where he was yesterday. Cheeky young brat from what I hear.' Quite unexpectedly he smiled. 'I told you he'd got spirit.'

'I want the boy brought to the jetty within the next ten minutes. The Captain here wants to see his son.'

'Fair enough,' said Chou and disappeared.

'Now, you come with me!' Lin Pao ordered.

Captain Lee followed the pirate down on to the main deck, where he stopped and looked around. Two pirates pushed past carrying a heavy drum of paint.

'What's going on!' Captain Lee exclaimed. 'What are you people doing?'

They were surrounded by a hum of activity. Captain Lee rushed to the ship's side and peered over. Below him, wooden planks were suspended on ropes, along the length of the hull. Men with long brush handles were hard at work. The *Serota Star*'s faded yellow sides were already a patchwork of new black paint. Someone had spilt some across the deck in front of them. A trail of smeary footprints led forwards.

There was a warning shout from above. Captain Lee put a hand to his eyes and saw the blue flash of oxy-acetylene torches at work, high up on the funnel. The pirates had almost finished cutting through the welds holding the shipping company's logo in place. It hung drunkenly for a moment then fell with a loud clang on to the deck below.

Furious, Captain Lee turned on Lin Pao. 'You vandals!' he shouted. Chou appeared from nowhere and stood very close. Captain Lee took a deep breath and turned away.

'All ready,' Chou told Lin Pao and led the way to the bows.

By the time they got there, Captain Lee had his feelings back under control.

Lin Pao pointed. 'Your son!' he said, politely.

The waiting boys looked up at the bows of the *Serota Star*.

'How old are you?' Duc To asked.

'Thirteen. You?' Tom replied.

'Twelve.'

'My name is Tom. Tom Lee.' He put out his hand rather self-consciously. 'Do you live here too?'

Duc To shrugged. 'I've been here three years, if that's what you mean. I'm Vietnamese. I'm a slave like you.'

Tom gasped. A slave? Was that what he was? No! He shook his head vigorously. The boy had got it all wrong! What had that man Chou told him? 'You're a hostage. If your father does the business, you'll be OK.' He turned to Duc To, eager to put him right. But his mind was racing ahead. What if his father failed? If something went wrong? What if the pirates broke their word? He had not thought about that. Then he could be here for ever!

'Look!' Duc To pointed.

Tom saw his father standing in the ship's bows. He was wearing his uniform cap with the gold braid across the peak and looked his usual smart self. The sight of him reassured Tom. His father would not fail whatever they gave him to do. He'd be fine. Tom gave a loud yell and waved frantically. His father waved back. Great, thought Tom in huge relief. It was going to be all right after all. They'd both soon be leaving here.

Abruptly, his father turned away. A brief parting wave and he disappeared into the crowd of men on the ship's deck.

'We saw you yesterday,' Duc To said. 'Nancy and me. You were washing dishes.'

'I know. I saw you too.'

There was a pause. 'Where do you live?' Tom asked.

Duc To turned and pointed towards the green fringe of the jungle. 'In a hut. It was empty. No one lived there so I moved in.'

'I slept on a bench last night. In the cookhouse,' Tom told him. 'It was rotten. There were rats everywhere. I heard them squeaking all night long.'

'The pirates say the cook gives them rats to eat.'

'I hate the cook,' Tom said bitterly.

Duc To nodded. 'I had to work for him when I first came. Then they put me on Chou's boat. The cook's terrified of Chou. He'll do anything to suck up to him. Tell you what,' he said after a moment's thought. 'Come and sleep in my hut. There's lots of room.'

Tom brightened. 'Great. Thanks! Which one is it?'

They walked through the village towards the jungle. A group of children were getting ready to play basketball.

'There's no point being friendly with them,' Duc To told him as Tom called 'Hi!' to a couple of them.

'They're pirates' children. They ignore us. They think we're scum.'

'Who's "us"?'

'You, me and Nancy.' He dropped his voice. 'She works for the Dragon Lady. She's the boss here. She's very old and everyone's frightened of her. Even Lin Pao and Duang.'

'Who's Duang?'

'One of the captains. Same as Lin Pao.'

'Who's worse?'

Duc To looked at him. Puzzled. 'They both are. In different ways.'

Tom said nothing.

'You're not scared of snakes, are you?' Duc To asked. 'Only, there're a couple in the thatch. They go after the rats. You can hear them at night when they're hunting.'

Tom shivered. 'No. Not really.'

'They won't come down,' Duc To assured him. 'They're frightened of us. It's different in the jungle though.' And he started to click his tongue.

The hut was small and bare. It was made entirely from palm fronds and leaves. There was an old bamboo mat on the floor and a chair in one corner.

'It's not very comfortable,' Duc To said shyly.

'It's great!' enthused Tom. 'Thank you!'

He heard his name being shouted.

'That's the cook,' Duc To told him. 'No one likes him. But he's not as tough as he pretends. But you'd better go. Watch him when he's drunk!' he called after Tom.

Chapter 21

Tom was bored. Cleaning the tables after the pirates had eaten their midday meal was not his idea of fun. He had discovered that half the pirates lived and fed with their families while the others ate here. The mess hall was a long, thatched building that was open at one end. Inside, there were half a dozen wooden tables and a number of rickety chairs.

At the other end, an old army burner had been dug into the ground. At mealtimes, a jet of flame roared away under a row of battered iron cooking pots. Here, the cook presided over his little empire, holding a large ladle which was his badge of office.

Tom wiped the tabletops down with a piece of old rag. The cracks in the tables had long ago been filled with rice and grey flakes of fish. This seemed to be the pirates' staple diet. All the table legs stood in tins of varying sizes. The tins were full of water to keep the ants away. One of Tom's early morning jobs was to keep them filled.

He finished the last table and began arranging the chairs for supper. He was in no hurry to finish. The next job was by far the worst. Cleaning out the cooking pots and containers with river sand was revolting. The smell was disgusting and by the time he had finished, his hands and arms were covered with a horrible, greasy scum. No one here used soap. Or toothpaste. He had never ever felt so dirty in all his life. He had asked Duc To last night, where he could get soap from. The boy had thought it very funny. Tom knew what his mother would have said.

There was a shout behind him. The cook was back. Tom turned to face the open doorway. He had learnt quickly that it didn't pay to let the man get too close. He had a kick like a mule and Tom had the bruises to show for it. Tom kept a wary eye on him.

'You picked up the rubbish from the big house yet?' the cook yelled.

Tom looked at him blankly. 'What "big house"?'

The cook swore. 'Up on the hill! The Dragon Lady. You idiot!'

Tom threw the rag down at the man's feet. 'You

never told me to! You're the idiot, not me!'

The cook's face darkened. 'Get up there now! You lazy brat!'

Tom stood his ground. 'Then what? I'm not a mind-reader!'

'You throw it on the dump!' the cook screamed. 'In the jungle. Follow the track from the foot of the steps.'

He came closer and stuck his face into Tom's. His teeth were crooked and stained. His breath stank. Tom recoiled.

'Know something?' the cook asked with a nasty leer. 'When your father's gone, I'm going to make your life hell! Got it? I'm going to put you in the cage!'

Tom glared at him in disgust.

'Now, get the rubbish!'

It was a long climb to the top of the steps. Tom stopped to get his breath back and looked around. Some way below, the *Serota Star*, now repainted black and almost unrecognizable, lay at anchor. In front of him, there was a pleasant-looking bungalow, well screened by trees. A wide veranda ran around the front of it. He walked up the five wooden stairs towards an open door. And stopped.

A girl had appeared. She was small and thin and had

long black hair that came down to her waist. She came out to meet him.

'What are you doing here, boy?'

For a moment, Tom was nonplussed. 'I've come for the rubbish.'

The girl looked shocked. 'And about time too!' She wrinkled her nose. 'But you don't come to this door for the rubbish. Haven't you got any sense? Go round the back! That's where rubbish is kept.'

'Oh!' said Tom. 'I didn't know.'

She was peering at him with interest. 'You're the new boy? From the ship?'

'That's right. I'm Tom Lee.'

She brightened. 'You're the one in Duc To's hut?'

Tom nodded.

'I'm Nancy!'

A sharp, imperious voice cut across their conversation. 'Who's that out there?'

Nancy put a finger to her lips and began pushing Tom away. 'Quickly!' she mouthed. 'Go round the back.'

'I asked you who's there, girl!' came the voice again.

'Only a boy for the rubbish, ma'am,' Nancy told her. 'He's new.'

'Did you tell him about the python?'

'No, ma'am. I forgot!'

123

The Dragon Lady gave a cackle.

'Oh well, let's hope there're lots more boys! Now, go and get me a ripe mango. The ones in the fruit basket are still too green.'

Chapter 22

'If you're ready,' said the Dragon Lady, 'we should get on.' She banged the end of her cane on the floor.

They watched in silence as Nancy appeared and began gathering up the porcelain bowls and the teapot. Carefully, the girl carried the tray out of the room and closed the screen door after her.

The Dragon Lady cleared her throat. 'We'll start. Lin Pao! Is the ship ready for sea?'

Lin Pao made a little bow with his head. 'Yes, Lady! She has been repainted and renamed. We've called her *Azura*. She can be underway in one hour.'

'Fuel state?' she demanded.

'Her tanks are three-quarters full.'

'Enough to get to Canton,' Duang broke in.

She rapped the floor with her cane. 'You never change, do you, Duang? You assume all the time.

Assume nothing. Wait until you know for certain. Or else, one day it will be the death of you.'

Lin Pao's chair creaked as he sat further forward.

'Besides,' she snapped. 'It's not Canton. The Family want us to use a smaller port called Ping Lo. It's a hundred miles further north and safer for us. They have good contacts there. The ship will be met by friends who will arrange for the cargo to be offloaded. It's all in a letter I have prepared.'

She laid a hand on the package lying beside her on a small table. Lin Pao saw she was wearing her favourite emerald ring.

'They are chartering a fishing boat to bring our crew straight back here,' she told them. 'They will transfer to it immediately after arrival. Do you understand?'

Lin Pao and Duang nodded.

'Our friends will be expecting the ship to reach Ping Lo four days from now. That is the plan. Now, I must tell you, which one of you I have chosen to do this.'

Her bright little eyes fixed on Lin Pao. 'You are the senior man,' she began then broke off abruptly as Duang started to protest. She raised her stick at the man. There was an awkward silence before Duang lowered his eyes.

She glared at him, her face puckered in rage. 'As I

was saying! Lin Pao, you are the senior man. No one doubts that! But you are also a deserter.'

Lin Pao's heart sank.

The Dragon Lady's voice soothed. 'We Chinese have long memories, Lin Pao. If the authorities heard afterwards that you were in charge, they might hold it against the Family. That would cause trouble in the future. Disrespect is as bad as losing face.'

Lin Pao struggled to keep his feelings under control. He must not show any public anger at her choice of this great ox, Duang.

The Dragon Lady watched his face. Her eyes forced his to meet her. He looked into them and felt his soul laid bare. She had such power over him. Over them all.

She turned to Duang. 'This man. This Captain Lee. Is he likely to do anything stupid?'

While Duang considered, Lin Pao told her, 'Not as long as we have his son. He dotes on the boy.'

She nodded, satisfied. 'In that case, make sure the boy is on the jetty when Duang leaves. The boy should be very visible. I want Captain Lee to see him for as long as possible. Duang won't need Lee for the short run down river. The Captain should stay out on the bridge wing.'

'So what's his job when we're at sea?' Duang asked.

The Dragon Lady nodded. 'Good question, Duang. His job is very important. He is to act like a ship's pilot. He is to keep you in the correct shipping lanes. He will make sure you obey the rules of the road for big ships going through the Straits. His responsibility is to get you safely to Ping Lo. He has the necessary experience to do all that.'

She pointed a finger at him. 'Your job, Duang, is to make sure he does not trick us. If he does, your life will be finished.' She paused to let the threat sink in. 'And Duang,' she went on, speaking with deliberate emphasis, 'he must NEVER EVER have access to the radio room. Under pain of death. Not even if you were to escort him there yourself. Do you understand, Duang? He is an intelligent man. If he can trick you, he will.'

Duang bowed his head to hide his embarrassment.

'Make sure you tell him this, Duang, before you sail!' she insisted. 'And make doubly sure, he understands!'

'When do we sail?' Duang asked, hoarsely.

She looked at her watch. 'You leave here at 1700 hours and take your time going down river. It's narrow along there. Do not enter the Straits until dark. And only switch on your navigation lights when you are well away from the estuary. You are a good sailor,

Duang. You should have no problems.'

Duang flushed at the unexpected compliment. 'This man Captain Lee,' he asked, feeling emboldened. 'Is he going all the way with us?'

The Dragon Lady frowned. 'That has not yet been decided. You will be told.' She picked up the package and handed it to him. 'These are your instructions and all the information you need to know. Read it and understand every word. You will radio in here every morning and every night.'

She paused. 'There are also ten thousand American dollars for any emergency that might stop you getting to Ping Lo on time. You will, of course, be accountable to me for how it's spent.'

She looked at them both. 'Any final questions?'

The two men shook their heads.

'Good luck! You will soon both be rich men!'

They stood up and waited until she left the room.

Chapter 23

They sat in the darkness of the hut, talking in quiet voices. Outside, the night was loud with the sound of frogs calling to one another. Occasionally, the scream of an animal in pain reminded them that the jungle was only fifty metres away.

Duc To was smoking a cheroot he had found earlier that day in the *Ular Ular*'s cabin. It was one of Lin Pao's best. He and Nancy were sharing it. He had offered it to Tom who had taken one puff and then broken into a fit of coughing.

'It's good!' Nancy told him. 'And it keeps away mosquitoes.'

'I don't mind mosquitoes too much,' Tom replied. 'It's snakes that get me.'

As he spoke, there was a sudden rustling in the thatch overhead. Nancy brushed his bare arm with the tips of her fingers and giggled as Tom made a nervous start.

'Don't worry,' she said. 'They won't bite you. They're not the poisonous sort.'

Tom shivered and edged closer to the others. They sat in a half-circle facing the open hut entrance. Outside, the sky was full of stars, bright enough to send shadows from the palm trees slanting down towards the river and for them to see each other's faces.

'Tom's got nothing to worry about,' Duc To told Nancy. 'He's out of here in a couple of weeks. Lucky devil.' He sucked at the cheroot then handed it to her.

'Less,' said Nancy. 'If all goes to plan.'

Tom listened and drew some small comfort from what they were saying. It had been a long, miserable afternoon. He had watched the ship make her way down river, taking his father further and further away. He had never felt abandoned before. It was a cold, sinking feeling, especially when the ship finally disappeared from sight.

He listened to Duc To and Nancy's chatter and wondered when he'd see his father again. Nancy and Duc To said he would, but they weren't the people who mattered. What about the Dragon Lady? And that man, Duang?

Nancy nudged him. 'You're very quiet.'

Tom blinked. 'What happens if there's a problem at sea? What happens if things get messed up?'

'Then you'll have to stay here with us,' Duc To told him, sounding offhand. 'You'll get used to it. Won't he, Nancy?'

'Don't be a pig!' Nancy snapped. 'I've been here for years and I'll never get used to this place. I hate it!' She spoke in a fierce whisper.

'Have you ever tried to get away?' Tom asked.

Duc To laughed. There was a sneering, almost resentful tone to it.

'Where's there to escape to? Fancy a stroll through the jungle, do you? If you're lucky, maybe a python will crush you to death before it eats you. If you're not, it'll just swallow you alive.'

'Stop it, Duc To!' warned Nancy. 'Can't you see he's upset? He's just seen his father go off with Duang's bunch of cut-throats.' She put her arm around Tom's shoulder. 'Duc To's been here too long,' she told him. 'He'll become one of them if he's not careful. You wait and see.'

'Yes, but has anyone tried to escape?' insisted Tom.

'I've just told you, haven't I? You stupid or something?' Duc To snapped. 'There's no way out through the jungle. You'd be lost in ten minutes.'

'Well, down the river, then,' said Tom stubbornly.

Duc To gave a short laugh. 'Oh yes! Please, Mr Lin Pao,' he mimicked. 'Can I borrow your boat?' He laughed sarcastically. 'Or perhaps you're thinking of clinging to a passing log? I mean, there's only sharks and crocodiles out there.'

'I'd take one of those fishing boats.'

'And have Lin Pao come after you with a machine gun? Shove it, Tom! You're talking rubbish.'

'You can't do it, Tom,' Nancy told him. 'I've thought about it for years. Duc To's right. There is no way out.' She nudged him. 'Anyway, you're not going to be here that long.'

'Long enough for a stretch in the cage,' Duc To joked. 'Especially if the cook has anything to do with it.'

'That pig!' Nancy agreed. 'I'd like to see him get what he deserves.'

'Me too!' agreed Duc To. 'One day he'll get it.'

'Like what?' Tom challenged.

'Food poisoning?' Duc To suggested. 'Or maybe a snake in his bedding.'

'Don't you even think about it, Tom,' warned Nancy. 'He'd guess it was you. You'd be in the cage for sure.'

'What is this cage?'

'You don't want to know,' she said and asked, 'Is the cook really that bad?'

Tom nodded. 'Pretty bad. And now Dad's gone, he'll get worse.'

'He's a sicko!' said Nancy.

'A snake in the bed sounds good to me,' said Duc To, stubbing out the cheroot. 'Pity you don't like snakes! Now, it's bed for me. Lin Pao's got an inspection in the morning. Guess who he'll be picking on!'

Chapter 24

Sergeant Chung stifled a yawn and peered at his watch. Then he drew back into the shadow of the doorway. It would be dawn in a couple of hours.

'Time to take a look?' the Special Branch man beside him prompted.

A rat scurried along the top of a monsoon drain. It was the size of a cat. It crossed the steps that led up to Mr Patou's workshop and disappeared under a loose plank in the side of the next-door building.

Sergeant Chung looked up and down the road for the hundredth time then stared at the flight of stairs facing them. There was no cover at all. What if someone came along? The whole operation would be blown.

'There's not been a taxi for the past half-hour,' the Special Branch man reminded him.

He was right, Sergeant Chung thought. The cruising

taxis with their loads of drunken sailors had finally gone home. A juke-box was still playing somewhere. They could hear the dull thud of the bass. But the longer they stayed here, the greater the chance of someone coming by and spotting them.

Sergeant Chung made up his mind. 'OK!'

They ran across the dirty street, the Special Branch man leading. At the top of the stairs he disarmed the burglar alarm then bent to examine the door locks. He handed Sergeant Chung the torch.

'Easy!' he scoffed and pulled out a bunch of stainless steel key picks. Seconds later, they were inside. Sergeant Chung closed the door behind them, wincing as the hinges squealed. He held his torch at shoulder height and played it across the room.

A thousand eyes stared back at them. Eyes that glowed in the torch beam. The Special Branch man gave an involuntary gasp and edged to one side. Something soft landed on the floor beside him. In the light of the torch, they saw a giant teddy bear lying there with its arms outstretched towards them.

They threaded their way past the rows of small tables with their sewing-machines and bundles of fabric. The air was heavy with the smell of cheap scent and cooking oil. There were pin-ups of boy bands taped to the walls. At the far end of the room, there was a door marked 'Strictly Private' in both English and Chinese.

Sergeant Chung tried the handle. It was locked.

'Child's play!' the Special Branch man told him.

Inside, they saw a cheap wooden desk and, close by, a huge steel safe. There were a number of old filing cabinets along one wall and, facing the desk, a modern fax machine.

'That's some safe!' Sergeant Chung groaned.

'Mid-twentieth-century technology,' the Special Branch man scoffed. 'What d'you want me to do first?'

'The safe,' Sergeant Chung told him. 'Then you can bug their fax.'

The man nodded. 'Shine the torch on the dial.'

'How long will it take?'

'Twenty minutes. Maybe more. Maybe less.' He patted his pockets and pulled out a doctor's stethoscope. 'Need to hear the tumblers falling.' He put a finger to his lips and knelt down. He was soon engrossed.

Sergeant Chung waited patiently. He listened to the rats scurrying across the floor outside, their toenails click-clicking on the wooden floorboards. There was a low munching sound somewhere above his head. It was either a deathwatch beetle or termites. Probably termites, he decided.

The Special Branch man grunted and sat back on his heels. He began to spin the dial in the middle of the safe, first one way and then the other. His face was rigid with concentration. There was a faint thud and the door swung open.

'Bingo!' cried Sergeant Chung. He patted the man on the back and gave him the torch. 'Your turn. Let's see what he keeps in here!'

Expertly, he began to search. There were thick bundles of old bank statements and invoices from suppliers. There were orders from overseas customers and tax demands. Mr Patou was a good businessman whatever his criminal tendencies. But that seemed to be all there was. Disappointed, Sergeant Chung was about to start putting everything back, when a thin plastic folder slipped out from inside a pile of fabric catalogues. Sergeant Chung pulled it out and flipped it open. He gave a whoop of triumph.

'What is it?' the Special Branch man hissed. He grabbed Sergeant Chung's arm. 'Tell me!'

Sergeant Chung's hands were trembling. He laid the folder on the floor and with great care pulled out a single sheet of flimsy paper. Silently, he pointed to the shipping company logo and address and at the blocks of figures underneath.

'It's the information on the *Serota Star*! The stuff from head office!' His voice trembled. 'It's exactly the same fax they sent my wife. We've got him. Redhanded!'

Chapter 25

Tom was in a bad mood. He was never at his best first thing in the morning and today had started badly. Duc To must have forgotten to wake him, he decided, as he ran across the grass towards the cookhouse. It was already light by the time he got there. A couple of pirates were waiting for their early morning mug of tea. They were the ones who went out fishing every morning, and what they caught made up the tastiest part of the day's meals. They also became very impatient if things were not ready for them. It was Tom's job to light the cooker and heat the water.

Tom rushed past, ignoring their grumbles. He heard the roar of flame from the cooker and saw the cook busily stirring in a packet of sugar. The cook looked up, saw Tom and started to yell at him.

'Oh shut up!' Tom shouted back.

This infuriated the cook. He sprang towards the boy and began jabbing at his chest with a dirty forefinger.

'Hey! Back off!' Tom protested, holding up his hands in mock surrender.

This inflamed the man more still. He lashed out at Tom with his fist. Tom ducked but couldn't avoid the knee that caught him hard on the leg. The pain took his breath away and he instinctively bent to clutch it. The cook cursed him and slapped his face.

Tom saw the iron ladle. He reached for it, swung it back over his shoulder and hit the cook as hard as he could on the side of his head. The cook yelled in outrage, staggered back and tripped over the tea container. The boiling water tipped over his shins and feet. He began screaming.

Now there were people everywhere, shouting at Tom, at the cook, at each other. Someone was hauling the man to his feet. Others fussed over the container, more concerned with how much was left.

'What the hell's going on?' shouted Chou in fury. He grabbed Tom by the shoulder and spun him round. 'What have you done?' The cook began to wail, loudly.

'He kicked me! He attacked me!' Tom protested. 'So I banjoed him with this!' And he brandished the ladle for Chou to see.

One of the pirates shouted, 'The boy's right!' The others were demanding tea and arguing amongst themselves. The cook was clutching his shins and sobbing loudly.

Chou pointed at the cook. 'Chuck him in the river! It'll cool him off!' Then he turned and glared at Tom. 'Same for you! Only worse!' He beckoned to a couple of men. 'Put him in the cage!'

Strong arms seized the boy and rushed him outside.

'Hey! Wait! It's not fair!' Tom shouted, but no one paid any attention. He tried to struggle but it was hopeless. He let his body sag but it made no difference. They dragged him through the sand down to the water's edge.

There was something in the river ten metres off shore. It looked like a fish trap. Something like that. He started shouting again as they pulled him towards it. By the time they reached the heavy bamboo cage, he was waist deep in water. Without warning, they ducked him. Tom came up retching and quite unable to resist as they pushed him inside. They slid the entrance shut and dropped an iron bar in place to secure it.

'Remember to keep your head above water!' one of the pirates shouted as they splashed away. The others laughed.

Chapter 26

Sergeant Chung couldn't help smiling. 'This is it, sir. This is their copy of the fax my wife received concerning the *Serota Star*.'

The Commissioner took it and carefully laid the sheet of paper on his desk. He stared at it in almost disbelief. 'You took this from Patou's safe?'

Sergeant Chung nodded. He indicated the man standing beside him. 'Special Branch here opened the safe. He was with me all the time.'

The Commissioner blew out his cheeks in amazement. 'And you're absolutely sure this is an exact copy?'

Sergeant Chung nodded vigorously. 'It's what their bug was there for. To access our secret information. Or rather, the shipping company's.'

'We also found a code book at the bottom of one of his filing cabinets,' Special Branch added.

'We've double-checked everything.'

The Commissioner tapped the fax in front of him. 'Bit of a risk taking this from Patou's safe, isn't it?'

'Not really, sir.' Sergeant Chung shook his head. 'This information is over a week old. And now, they've already hijacked the ship. I can't see him needing to read it all over again.'

The Commissioner sat back in his chair and put his fingertips together. 'So what does all this give us?'

'Quite a lot,' Sergeant Chung told him. 'It confirms that Patou knew all about the *Serota Star*'s movements. Where she was docking and when. What she was carrying and its value. And he knew how and where all this information was coming from.'

'Then he passed it all on to the Triad family concerned?'

The Special Branch man agreed. 'Yes. Whoever they are.'

'But we don't know that yet?'

'No.'

'Patou's telephone and fax are now bugged,' Sergeant Chung went on.

'We'll hear something soon enough,' reassured the Special Branch man.

The Commissioner frowned. 'We've still got to find the ship.'

'And Captain Lee and his son, Tom,' Sergeant Chung put in quietly. 'I gather that Mrs Lee's in a bad way. Not surprising. She's on her way down here as a guest of the Company. My wife's meeting her at the airport this afternoon.'

The Commissioner got to his feet. 'This man, Patou, needs twenty-four-hour, round-the-clock surveillance. I want to know who he talks to. What he says. Where he goes and who visits him.' He broke off and looked at the Special Branch man. 'Don't we have anything on him at all?'

The man made a tilting motion with his hand. 'Lots of rumours and hearsay but nothing factual. We think we know who some of his contacts might be. He meets people in a dockside joint called Garry's Bar. I'll check that out too.'

'Good!' said the Commissioner.

'One other thing, sir!' the Special Branch man went on. 'How was it that the pirates knew exactly which ship to go for? We know from Mrs Chung's office that she was in regular touch with the *Serota Star* right up until the ship was halfway up the Straits. Then it all went quiet.'

'That must have been when the pirates attacked,' Sergeant Chung told him.

The Special Branch man nodded. 'Which was at night-time. So just how did they know which ship to go for? I mean, there were no other reports that other vessels had been threatened. Funny, isn't it?'

The Commissioner looked puzzled. 'You mean the ship was "bugged"?'

'Something like that,' said the Special Branch man slowly.

'How do you "bug" a ship?' the Commissioner asked.

'You use a radio direction transmitter,' Sergeant Chung told him. 'It's a device that sends out its own radio signal.'

'And someone with a receiver tuned to the same frequency can, in theory, intercept it and home in on it,' the Special Branch man said, thoughtfully. 'Wasn't Captain Lee's ship having problems with her radio before she reached Singapore?'

'And my wife organized the repair,' nodded Sergeant Chung. 'I think she said the technicians were new to her and very efficient.'

'I think we should have them checked out too,' said the Commissioner. 'Right then! Let's get on with it!'

Chapter 27

The tide was coming in. Tom had first noticed it half
an hour ago. Now, it was creeping remorselessly
upwards. If he stood on the bamboo floor of the cage,
the water reached the bottom of his ribs. If he climbed
up the side of the cage, it dropped back to his knees.
He couldn't go any higher without banging his head on
the top of the cage. He could put his arms through the
gaps but not his head. There was not enough room to
thrust a head through. The cage had been deliberately
built to prevent that.

He stood looking at the riverbank, staring at the
high-water mark. He could see the line of flotsam and
bleached pieces of wood clearly enough. What was
much harder to decide was how much lower down in
the river the cage actually was. There was no obvious
tidemark on the smooth bamboo poles. As the tide

climbed higher, the more worried he became.

He tried to be rational. He talked out loud to reassure himself. The pirates weren't going to let him drown? Why would they? What would be the point? The deal was that his father would take the ship to wherever they wanted it taken. Then, they would both be released. So why should they want to drown him? Like a rat in a trap?

He felt the water reach his armpits and shuddered. The tide was coming in fast. He climbed up as far as he could to get away from it. He pressed his face against the underside of the bars and stared up at the sky. Surely the water wouldn't get as high as this? 'Like a rat in a trap,' his brain kept repeating . . . 'a rat in a trap.'

The water became noticeably colder as it got deeper. And yet, the sun continued to beat down on his head. His mouth was strangely dry and he wanted to drink. He remembered his mother's warnings about drinking dirty water and clung to that memory with a fierce determination not to let her down.

He heard the buzz of an outboard engine. A fishing boat came into view. A tall pirate in a red shirt was standing in the stern with one hand on the tiller. Tom watched a dark line in the river coming towards him and cried out in surprise as the boat's wake splashed over his face. He rubbed at his mouth and eyes with one hand. The sound of the engine faded and he was on his own again. A boy in a cage, in a river where the water was now over his shoulders.

He looked towards the riverbank and cried out loud in panic. He could clearly see the tidemark. So the water was still rising! He tried to make himself think of other things. His father would be out in the Straits by now with the men who had thrown poor Robert overboard. And didn't that seem a long, long time ago?

The water was touching his chin! His legs and stomach were cold. He started to shiver. It became uncontrollable. His teeth were chattering. He looked around in panic. There was nothing to see. There was no one there for him. He began to shout. Louder and increasingly desperate. He cursed the pirates. He cursed his god. He started shouting for his parents.

There was a cloud near the sun. Slowly, the surface of the river darkened. A small breeze began to ruffle the surface. The colours drained from the jungle and soon everything was grey and forbidding. It took an age for the cloud to go over. When it did, and the sun came out again, some of Tom's optimism returned with the gleam and sparkle on the water.

But there was more good news. He realized suddenly

that the tide was stationary. Perhaps even falling! By how much, he couldn't decide. A centimetre? Not much more than that. But falling it definitely was. He stopped shivering. A growing sense of elation seized him. Even if they kept him out here until the next high tide, he knew he could handle it. He knew now what to expect. And then he saw the snake.

It was about five metres away. A yellow and black banded sea snake. An ular. A member of the cobra family and very poisonous. It swam with its head out of the water, its unwinking eyes looking directly at him!

Tom's mouth worked and he could hear himself trying to be sick. The snake was swimming in lazy zigzags. Close enough now for him to see its tongue, flickering in and out. Three metres away and coming straight for the cage. There was water dripping from its outstretched neck. A terrible determination gripped him. He was not going to die of snakebite in a horrible place like this. Not without a fight!

He took a deep breath and threw himself into the water, splashing and beating at it with outstretched arms. He opened his eyes underwater and searched for the snake. He thought he saw its tail twisting away. He surfaced and looked wildly in its direction. There was no sign of it. He flung his back against the side of the cage and began splashing with his legs.

How long it went on for, he had no idea. There was no such thing as time. He was alone and living with his worst nightmare. There was no sign of the snake here on the surface but what if it was coming up for him from the depths? He scanned the river on all sides and thrust his head under the surface trying to see.

Sometime later, he found he could stand up easily. The water level was down now to below his stomach and falling quickly. He stopped splashing. It was clear that the snake had gone and, besides, he was too tired to continue. But he had beaten the snake and was proud of himself for that. As he relaxed, exhaustion overwhelmed him. His head felt too heavy for his shoulders and kept falling forwards. His eyes closed. He had never been this tired before. But he had won. He had survived the cage.

There was something else he was certain about. He must keep away from the cook. Duc To had warned him about the man. And his knife. After this morning's public humiliation, Tom knew the cook would be looking for revenge. He would have to be extra careful from now on. The realization greatly depressed him. Eventually, he fell into a doze. He was aware of the river draining away from around his knees and the sound it made streaming through the bars of the cage.

As the sun was going down, he dreamt he could hear voices. He woke up when Chou stooped over him and lifted the boy on to his shoulders. He thought he heard the pirate say, 'You're one of my crew now, lad.' But he was probably only dreaming.

Later that night, he heard his name being called. It was a girl's voice, very soft but insistent. Tom sat up. It was Nancy. Carefully, he got to his feet. He did not want to wake Duc To who was sleeping soundly nearby.

Nancy seized him by his hand and led him a little way from the hut. 'Oh Tom!' she whispered. 'Are you all right? Was it terrible in there? Poor Tom.' To his surprise, she flung her arms around his neck and hugged him. 'I was so worried but they wouldn't let me come.'

'I'm OK,' said Tom shyly.

'You're very brave,' she told him. 'And popular. Everyone thinks it was great the way you hit the cook.'

'But I didn't mean to scald him like that,' Tom protested.

She squeezed his hand. 'Let them believe what they want. It'll make your life much easier. And I'm so proud of you. A lot of grown men couldn't have done what you did today.'

She reached up and kissed his cheek. The next moment, she was gone.

Chapter 28

The next morning, Tom woke very early. He could only hear one of the village cockerels crowing. Soon, all the others would join in. Until then, he was going to enjoy the sense of everything being quiet and at rest. Duc To was still asleep. The boy lay on his side, cradling his head with an arm. His breathing was scarcely audible.

Tom stared up at the roof and thought about the last twenty-four hours. There was a lot to remember. He was surprised to find he felt much the same as ever despite what had happened. He did not feel traumatized in any way because of it. That was good! His leg was sore, though, and stiff. It would be painful walking on it. That damn cook!

It was all his stupid fault. If he hadn't been such a bully and a control freak, none of this would have happened. The fight, the cage, the sea snake, none of it. And Nancy? What about her? Tom didn't know much about girls. He had not met many. But he was glad she liked him. She was somehow different from any of the others he had met.

He sat up and gave his head a good scratching. He felt wide awake now and keen to get on with the day. He grabbed his shorts and T-shirt and limped outside to dress. It was good to have the place to himself. He could think more clearly when it was like this. He looked around at the scattered huts. A dog lifted its leg at the entrance to one of them then trotted busily away. Tom walked down to the jetty where the two pirate boats were moored on either side. The machine guns, the long whip aerials and their waspish, black-painted hulls gave them an air of menace that was impossible to ignore. He wondered how fast they could go.

Lin Pao's boat was the sleeker of the two. She was moving in the current, tugging at her mooring ropes as if impatient to be out at sea doing her dreadful work. For some reason, he reached out and touched her side. Strange to think she was real. That men like Lin Pao and the cook actually existed and that he, Tom, was somehow caught up in their world. It almost seemed like a dream.

But the cage had been real enough. He could walk along the river this very moment and find it. He could even wade out and get back inside! A dreadful thought struck him and he groaned out loud. Was he expected back in the cookhouse? Was he still working for that man? Why did he think it was all over?

'Tom Lee!' a voice was shouting. He looked over his shoulder and saw Chou. He ran stiff-legged towards the pirate.

'How you feeling?' Chou asked in an almost friendly voice.

Tom nodded in surprise. 'Fine!'

The pirate laughed and put an arm around his shoulders. 'No hard feelings, then?'

Tom shook his head. 'I was a bit out of order,' he mumbled.

'Out of order?' The remark amused Chou. He gave a guffaw of laughter. 'You're all right, Tom Lee.' And he ruffled Tom's hair. 'But watch your back!'

They walked together towards the cookhouse. Tom could see people already there sitting at the tables.

'You start work after breakfast,' Chou told him as they went in. 'Haven't forgotten, have you? Chipping paint.'

A grin spread across Tom's face. Brilliant! So he had

been right after all. No more cookhouse for him! A warm, fuzzy feeling of contentment spread through him. The cook looked up and scowled. He was also walking with a limp. Tom followed Chou to a table. Other pirates joined them. Most looked curiously at Tom. One or two of them actually nodded at him, then ignored him completely.

Tom didn't mind. For the first time since he had been brought here, he was not miserable. He didn't know how long it would last, let alone if he should feel like this. But he did.

Chou was getting up. He looked down at the boy.

'At the boat in ten minutes! Don't be late!'

Chapter 29

Captain Lee adjusted his binoculars and scowled. One of the pirates must have been using them. They were a long way out of focus. He scanned the horizon again and this time he could see everything in sharp relief. He made a mental note to keep them with him at all times.

It was good to be back at sea. Very good. He regretted the thought the very next moment. Memories of his wife and poor Tom crowded into his mind, silently rebuking him for such selfishness. But then, he reasoned, the sooner he got this cargo to Ping Lo, the sooner they'd all be reunited. So therefore it was good for him to be back at sea. And that made him feel a little better.

He paced up and down the bridge wing, happy to leave Duang in charge. The man was slouched in the captain's chair with his feet up. Playing at being captain, he thought contemptuously. He scanned the sea ahead of them. There was bad weather coming. He could smell it. The wind was getting up and the sea had a dull, glassy colour to it. There might even be a typhoon coming.

They were halfway down the Straits, heading for Singapore and the wide expanses of the South China Sea beyond. In another twelve hours, they would be going through the Straits at their narrowest part. Meanwhile, he reminded himself, the world's third-largest oil tanker was barely a mile behind them. And if that didn't concentrate the mind, nothing else could.

He looked at his watch and wondered what his wife would be doing. And Tom as well. God! How he hated having to leave the boy behind. Some father, he was! All he could do was to hope and trust in the boy's common sense to stay out of harm.

There was rain coming on the wind. His forehead was damp. He went back into the bridge. Duang looked up as he pulled the door shut behind him. A telephone rang in the central console.

'Get it!' Duang ordered.

Captain Lee picked it up. 'Bridge! Captain speaking!'

'Chief engineer here!' came the reply. 'It's that main

bearing I told you about. It's running hot again!'

Captain Lee swore silently, aware of Duang's hostile gaze. He had to think quickly. If there had only been him involved, he would have told the chief to ignore the problem. Let it glow red hot. Anything to frustrate the pirates' plans. But it wasn't as simple as that. He was not on his own. There was Tom to consider. He couldn't take risks so long as Tom was a hostage.

He looked towards Duang. 'A problem for you!' he called. 'The main bearing's running hot. What do you want the chief engineer to do?'

Duang cursed. 'What main bearing? What d'you mean? Who you trying to fool!' He began to shout.

Captain Lee heard him out. Then said, 'We can't slow down too much. We'd be a danger to traffic. We'll be through the Straits in twelve hours. Do we go for it?'

Duang banged his fist against a bridge window and shouted at him. 'I need to report this!'

'Meantime?' Captain Lee asked.

Duang waved him away.

Captain Lee shrugged and spoke into the phone. 'I think Mr Duang wants you to carry on as you are until further orders.'

Chapter 30

Mr Patou was in a high good humour. In front of him was an opened letter and beside it a cheque made out to himself for a large amount of money. It was from the American distributor of his Christmas soft toy range. He picked up the cheque and his smile grew wider. It was time, he was thinking, to give himself a little treat. A small indulgence in recognition of his business skills. Lunch today would be at the Royal Peacock Hotel. He'd have a good steak and a bottle of the best burgundy. His mouth began to water.

His secretary came in with his early morning cup of coffee. Mr Patou got to his feet and insisted on kissing her hand.

'Well, he's not kissing mine!' said the foreman sourly, when she told him.

Mr Patou opened the safe and took out his accounts

ledger. He reached for his calculator and began crunching numbers. When he had finished, he gave a small chuckle. He closed the book with a sigh of contentment and wondered how the other business was proceeding. The *Serota Star*! Now that was a name he would always remember. When the money for that particular transaction arrived then perhaps he really could retire to his dream villa in the hills.

He glanced at the calendar. The ship must be well on her way to China. Perhaps she had already arrived? It would be nice to know. He stood up and began to pace up and down his office. That was the trouble with the Family. They were not good communicators. They only told you what was happening when they wanted you to do something for them. And Mr Patou had an insatiable curiosity. On impulse he picked up the phone.

'Yes!' came the usual harsh voice.

'Hello. It's me! I was just wondering about . . . er . . . things,' he gulped. He knew he should not be doing this.

'What "things"?'

He hesitated. 'Well, ships and things like that!'

There was a pause. Then, 'No news!'

'Would you like to meet sometime? The usual place?'

'Place stinks!' said the voice and the phone went dead.

Damn! thought Mr Patou. He could kick himself. He should not have done that. They were so paranoid about everything. Well, he wasn't going to let it ruin his day. I'll have a half-bottle of champagne to start with, he decided. The thought cheered him.

'Gotcha!' exclaimed Sergeant Chung ten minutes later when the monitoring unit had made their report. By then they had traced the telephone number Mr Patou had dialled and had identified the speaker at the other end.

'I know him!' Sergeant Chung told them excitedly. 'He's a Dragon! Let's share the good news with our friends at Special Branch. Then they can really put the Family under the microscope!'

Chapter 31

Tom knelt in the bows of the *Ular Ular* chipping paint. Every now and then, he stood up to ease the aching muscles in his back. His hair was thick with rust and paint flakes. He held a heavy hammer in one hand and a wide-bladed chisel in the other. Earlier that morning, Chou had shown him the rust around the base of the machine gun mounting.

'I want it finished today. Start it when you've done the deck.'

Chou was a hard taskmaster. Immediately after breakfast, he marched Tom down to the boat, thrust a large scrubbing-brush and a bucket at him, and said, 'Use clean sand on the deck and make sure you give it a proper scrub. If it's not up to scratch, you'll do it again! I'll be back later.'

The first hour was the worst. Tom was on all

fours scrubbing hard. Beads of sweat dripped steadily from his eyebrows. Muscles he never knew he had twisted in complaint. When he had finished, he lowered the bucket over the side and threw water over the main deck.

'Not bad!' Chou told him. And seeing the boy's expression, laughed. 'That's only the start.' He pointed to the bridge. 'Do that next. I want it spotless! Deck, lockers, windshield. There's a cupboard down below with rags and things. Find them!'

'Can I have a drink, please?' Tom asked.

'What do you think the river's for? Just get on with it! You'll be doing this for the next couple of weeks. So you'd better get used to it!' Chou grinned and walked down the jetty, whistling.

Tom wondered what was worse. Working in a greasy, disgusting kitchen with that evil cook on his back? Or this? Slowly, as the morning went by, his body adjusted. Working on the boat was far more tiring but at least he was on board a boat. And an amazing boat at that. And besides, he was beginning to pace himself and divide his work into manageable sections. And that made everything easier.

He wondered what his father was doing. He guessed the ship would be a long way down the Straits by now.

He thought about Duang and tried to imagine how his father was getting on with the man. Tom knew his father would be worrying about his own crew. They were all supposed to be freed at the end of the voyage. But would they be? He had a bad feeling about that.

With a stab of guilt, he thought of his mother. And felt sick! Poor old Mum! He could picture her sitting in the kitchen, waiting for news. She must know what had happened to her family. So she'd be dreading the worst. And he had hardly given her a thought since all this happened. That was terrible. He wondered who'd be comforting her and supposed Mrs Wen might.

Grimly, he went on with his work. He finished cleaning the windscreen that ran across the front of the bridge. He peered at it carefully to make sure he had not left any smeary marks. Chou had warned him about that. Satisfied, he stood up, took a deep breath and looked around. There was no one to be seen. He glanced up at the sky and decided it must be mid-afternoon. The pirates would be taking a nap. He wondered where Duc To was? He had seen him earlier that day on board Duang's boat. He had not been looking happy.

Tom called his name several times but there was no sign of the boy. He scratched his head and thought about Duc To. Things were not going so well between them. And now Tom had taken his place on board the *Ular Ular*. It wasn't Tom's fault but he knew Duc To would not see it that way. Duc To would feel he had been demoted. Then there was Nancy! He felt guilty about her too. After all she was Duc To's friend and not his. He almost wished she would ignore him. Almost. He was looking forward to seeing her later tonight when they all met up.

He leant over the bridge and stared at the river, looking for sea snakes. As he watched, a tree branch swept by and for the first time he noticed how fast the tide was going out. Water was splashing up at the boat's bows as the tide flowed down river towards the estuary. The mooring lines were at full stretch. Tom went up into the bows, reached down and gripped one. It was as rigid as an iron bar. He could feel it quivering under the strain. If anyone cast them off now, the *Ular Ular* would be swept out of sight in a matter of minutes.

He sat on his haunches and considered. Roughly speaking, the tide took six hours to go out and six hours to come back in. So in twelve hours' time, the flow should be just as strong. That would be about three o'clock in the morning. Tom snorted. To think Duc To had been here all these years and had not worked it out for himself! It was the obvious way to escape. It would certainly be the way he would choose. All one needed to do then was to get well clear of the village before starting the engine.

That should be easy enough! He thought about it for a while longer then realized that he was being unfair. He might know a lot about boat engines – that was his hobby – but Duc To didn't.

The *Ular Ular* had a superb engine. Earlier that morning, he had topped up her fuel tank. Chou had taken him to the end of the jetty and shown him the hut where the pirates kept their fuel stocks. 'We've no pump,' Chou had told him. 'All the stuff comes from the mainland in five-gallon jerricans. Your job is to keep her tank full.' It was a good fifty metres from the hut to the boat and Tom thanked his lucky stars he only had to heave one can back to the boat.

There was still no sign of anyone, so he climbed back on to the bridge. It felt great up here! He had an appreciative look around then took the wheel between his hands. He looked directly over the machine gun towards the jungle-covered hill on the far bank. In his mind he could hear the roar of the engine and feel the spray on his cheeks. It must be fantastic to go to sea in something as fast as this. He wondered what the *Ular*'s top speed might be. Thirty miles an hour? Forty? Fantastic!

He gazed at the instrument panel in front of him. The pirates seemed to have everything: radar, satellite navigational system, even a depth recorder. There was also something he had never seen before: a large dial with the words 'Radio Direction Finder' above the maker's name. Someone had scrawled '88.1' in grease pencil on the screen. Tom guessed it was for targeting ships.

There was no key in the ignition. Only Lin Pao would have that. He wondered where the man was. He had not seen him all day. Tom knelt down and peered up at the control panel. He began tracing his way through the maze of different-coloured wires. It was a lot like the electrical circuit on the *Serota Star*'s motor boat only there was so much more of it. The ignition system was easy enough to trace. A red plastic wire entwined with a green one. So, starting the boat was only a matter of touching the right wires together. The knowledge pleased him. It was somehow reassuring.

Chapter 32

Lin Pao disliked climbing the steps to the Dragon Lady's house at the best of times. It was even worse at night. He had read somewhere that mosquitoes can smell human sweat from thirty metres away. There were probably ten thousand of them within that distance now, and they were following him in a hungry cloud.

He also worried about treading on a snake. It had never happened yet but one of his crew had died from a bite the year before. There was no reason why a snake should be lying on any of the one hundred steps except, he reasoned, that they had to lie somewhere. He made a point of banging his feet down hard to warn them of his approach. He was very glad when he finally reached the veranda.

The child Nancy brought him a glass of mineral

water on a lacquered tray. Then left. He drank it without much enthusiasm. The Dragon Lady had strong views on alcohol. As she came in, he looked at her face and saw the spots of colour on her cheeks. So it was not good news.

'Two things to tell you, Lin Pao!' she exclaimed, as soon as the door shut behind her. 'Duang's got a problem.' She hobbled over to her chair and sat down.

He stared at her little wizened face and black beady eyes. He wanted to shout, 'Of course Duang has a problem! Duang always has a problem. And you preferred him to me!'

Outwardly, he remained impassive and waited to be told.

'The ship has a problem with a main bearing. Duang tells me it's running hot. They've been forced to reduce speed.'

Lin Pao listened in growing disbelief. 'Are we sure this isn't sabotage?' he demanded, trying hard to keep his voice under control.

She threw her hands up. 'Duang's questioned the engineers on board. It seems the same thing happened not long before we attacked her. It's possible, I suppose. Besides, we've got the boy here. His father knows if there's any monkey business, the boy will be killed.'

Lin Pao scowled. 'The only way to find out if these engineers are telling the truth is to take one and shoot him. They'll get it sorted out then, believe me!' He thought for a moment. 'Where's the ship now?'

'Still this side of Singapore,' she said furiously. 'And at this rate, it will take another week to reach port.'

'Can they repair the bearing?'

'Duang says the engineers think they can cope, so long as they stay at this slow speed. The Family,' she added, glancing at him, 'are not happy.'

Lin Pao was not surprised. 'Why don't I go and take a look? I could be there by dawn?'

The Dragon Lady shook her head. 'Duang's in charge. The Family want it that way.'

'Can't we divert her? Find another ship? Transfer cargo?'

'The Family are considering everything. We'll hear soon enough. I'll let you know.'

Lin Pao stood up. He bowed slightly and turned to go. At the screen door, he remembered.

'Lady, you said you had two things to tell me?'

She frowned then her brow cleared. 'Yes! This man, Lee. Captain Lee. The Family think it would be a mistake to let him go free. He is a skilled sailor. He almost certainly knows where this place is on the chart. We cannot take the risk! Duang will take care of him when they are close to Ping Lo. The boy must not know.'

There was the sound of something breaking inside the house. A plate or a glass, Lin Pao thought. Something like that.

The Dragon Lady shook her head angrily. 'That girl is getting so clumsy these days!'

Chapter 33

The lights were burning late in the Police Commissioner's office. 'I need an update,' he told them. 'And I've got the politicians on my back.' He paused to let the words sink in. 'This *Serota Star* business is about to go ballistic.'

Sergeant Chung looked sideways at the Special Branch man.

'You remember what her cargo's worth?' the Commissioner asked.

'Twenty million American dollars,' Sergeant Chung told him.

The Commissioner nodded. 'Well, not surprisingly, the Subishi Corporation's raising absolute hell about what's happened. It's putting pressure on our government to find the ship and to clear out these pirates once and for all.'

'Good!' said Sergeant Chung.

The Commissioner nodded. 'Starting tomorrow, the military is mounting a full-scale search for the ship. They're putting up aircraft and doubling the number of naval patrols. We've simply got to find her. It's becoming a matter of national honour!'

He took off his glasses and rubbed his eyes. 'Apparently, the media's got hold of the story. Mrs Lee's probably told someone. Not surprising, I suppose.' He looked at Sergeant Chung. 'How is she, by the way?'

Sergeant Chung made a face. 'Not bad, considering what's happened. But I don't know how long it will last.'

'I heard the shipping company is taking her off your hands tomorrow and keeping her out of the way,' the Special Branch man said.

'Right then!' said the Commissioner. 'Let's have your reports.'

'The Special Branch man cleared his throat. 'Not very much I'm afraid, sir.' He slid a pink-coloured file across the Commissioner's desk. 'This is the file we have on Patou's contact with the Dragon Family. He's a nasty bit of work. Suspected murder, kidnap, gross bodily harm. All the usual things.'

'Go on.'

'We've put spy cameras in the bar where he meets Patou and also in Patou's home and office.' He shook his head. 'We're watching all known Family members. We're still trying to find a way of bugging their places without them knowing. But it's not easy. They know all the tricks too.'

'Hell!' said the Commissioner.

'Why don't we just arrest them?' asked Sergeant Chung. 'And grill them?'

'That's being considered,' the Commissioner told him. 'Only trouble is there's a lot of politics involved here. The few Family bosses we know of are well-known legitimate business people. Celebrities, some of them. Then there're the others we know nothing about. The ones in the background. And they're the people who control everything.'

A depressing silence fell.

'What's your report, Chung?'

'Those technicians who repaired the ship's radio have disappeared. The firm they worked for has no idea where they are.'

'Sounds like another Family-owned enterprise to me,' the Special Branch man said cynically.

'Check the firm out,' the Commissioner ordered. 'It seems to tie in with your theory about the ship itself being bugged. I'd like a report from your technical people on how that type of bug actually works.' He blinked wearily. 'I know the problems you're up against but we've just got to get something definite on the *Serota Star*. Or my job's on the line along with yours. We either need a miracle or a smart piece of detective work. And you know what I'd prefer!'

Chapter 34

Nancy stood between the two boys and cried. Neither of them knew what was upsetting her. She had rushed into the hut, seen Tom standing there and promptly burst into tears. They put their arms around her shoulders and waited awkwardly for her to finish.

'Nancy! What is it? What's happened?' Duc To urged in a low voice.

In the village outside, people were getting ready for bed. A couple of radios were still playing but most of the pirates and their families had settled down for the night.

'Come on, Nancy,' said Tom, giving her arm a clumsy squeeze. 'It can't be that bad! Who's upset you?'

'Tom! Oh Tom!'

Duc To frowned.

'Just tell us what's happened,' Tom encouraged.

She wouldn't meet his eyes. 'It's too horrible! I can't.'

'Horrible for me?'

'No! Not you! Your father!'

He gaped at her. 'My father! What's he done?'

Nancy shook her head. 'He's done nothing! That's what makes it worse. Much worse!'

'Nancy! Just tell us, will you?' Duc To sounded angry.

Tom put his hands on her shoulders. Her skin was cold and she was shivering uncontrollably. 'Please, Nancy! You're frightening me.'

She bowed her head and they strained to hear what she said. 'The Dragon Lady told Lin Pao that the Family have ordered it!' She put her face in her hands and broke into more sobs.

'Ordered what?' cried Tom. 'Tell me!'

'Duang has orders to kill your father when they reach China.'

'Oh my God!' moaned Duc To. He folded his arms and began rocking back and forth.

Tom struggled to understand. It was unreal. Like acting in a play. This wasn't happening to him. He wanted to shout but the words stuck in his throat. His voice was hoarse. 'Why?'

'Because they think he knows where this place is,'

she told him, miserably. 'Then he can tell the police. So the soldiers will come and destroy it.' She wiped her nose on the back of her hand. 'She said you weren't to know.'

There was a long, long silence.

'The ship's got a problem,' she muttered. 'Something wrong with the engine. They're going to take much longer getting to China.'

Duc To put an arm around her waist. She pushed it away.

'Tom!' she pleaded. 'What do we do?'

'How long before the ship gets there?'

'To Ping Lo?' Nancy bit her lip. 'Five more days. That's what she told Lin Pao.'

Tom closed his eyes. Five days to do something. Five days to save his father.

'I'm really sorry, Tom,' Duc To began to say, when Tom interrupted.

'I can't just sit here and let it happen!'

'But what can you do?' Duc To cried impatiently. 'Look, Tom. I'm sorry for your father and for you. Very very sorry but . . .' His voice tailed off.

And that was the moment when Tom knew what he must do next.

'I know how to get out of here,' he told them.

'You what!' shouted Duc To. 'How can you? You've only just got here.' He went and stood beside Nancy. 'He's talking rubbish,' he said.

'Tom?' the girl gasped. 'You really mean that? You know a way out? How?'

'By boat. It's the only way!'

Chapter 35

'By boat! You're mad!' Duc To appealed to Nancy. 'He's crazy!' And he glared at Tom. There was no mistaking his hostility.

'You won't get as far as the estuary,' the boy scoffed. 'And even if you did, how long do you think you'll last at sea in one of those little fishing boats? You'll be swamped in minutes!' He laughed scornfully. 'That's if Lin Pao doesn't get you first with his machine gun.'

He grabbed Nancy's arm. 'It's gone to his head,' he sneered. 'Just because Chou likes him.' He glared at Tom. 'Now you're working on his boat, you think you know it all! Well, let me tell you. You're wrong. Dead wrong!'

Nancy touched Tom's hand. 'He's right, Tom! Those boats are so easy to turn over. You've got to be a proper fisherman to handle one.'

'I'm not planning on taking a fishing boat,' Tom told

them grimly. 'I'm taking *Ular Ular*. Lin Pao's boat!'

In the stunned silence that followed, the jungle sounded very loud. Instinctively, they all looked towards the hut entrance.

'He's joking,' Duc To told Nancy. 'Very funny, I don't think.'

Nancy hesitated. 'Tom?'

Tom shrugged. 'Look! I know it sounds crazy.'

'Crazy!' Duc To sneered. 'It's your death sentence. That's how crazy it is!'

'Maybe,' Tom agreed. 'But I know how to start the engine.'

'Without the key?'

Tom nodded. 'Without the key. I know a lot about boats and engines. I checked the wiring out this afternoon. I can start her.'

'But, Tom,' cried Nancy. 'They'll hear you. They'll be after you like a shot.'

Tom shook his head. 'Here's my plan. We cast off and let the tide take us down river to that big bend. Then, I'll start the engine . . .'

'And head out across the Straits!' Duc To interrupted, sarcastically.

'Right! There's a chart on board. And radar. I can handle it.'

'The radar's broken,' Duc To sneered. 'They're waiting for a spare part.'

'Then I'll need just the chart and a compass. Whatever!'

'Are you sure?' Nancy asked.

'Like, when?' Duc To scoffed.

'Tonight!' Tom said simply. 'I've got to go tonight! My dad's not got much time left. I've got to get help.'

Nancy clutched his arm. 'Can I come? Please?'

'We're all going, aren't we?' Tom frowned.

'Not me!' Duc To said angrily. 'No way!'

Nancy gave a little cry. 'But you must come. You've got to come, Duc To! It's what we've always talked about.'

'I'm not going with him!' Duc To went over to his bed mat and lay down with his back to them.

She followed Tom outside. 'You're sure it'll work?' she breathed.

He nodded. 'Pretty sure.'

'All right,' she gasped. 'When do we go?'

'Be here three o'clock tonight. And make sure no one sees you. If you're not here, I can't afford to miss the tide. I've only got one shot at this.'

'And if it fails?'

'Then there's not much future for either of us.'

Chapter 36

Tom woke with a start. For a moment he couldn't think where he was. Then memory came flooding back and he remembered what lay ahead. A cold hand seemed to clutch his heart and, for a moment, he felt sick. He pushed himself up and listened. He was lying just inside the entrance to the hut, well away from Duc To. He had done this deliberately to lessen the chances of accidentally waking the boy as he left. Tom peered at his watch. It was not easy to see. A scum of cloud now lay across the sky.

He thought it was twenty minutes to three. Only just in time! Cautiously, he got to his feet. He wondered if Nancy would come and began to hope she wouldn't. She could suffer badly because of him. What happened if someone saw her? Or if he couldn't get the engine started? He thought of his father. The pirates had betrayed him and hadn't the guts to tell him. Tom's resolve stiffened. He had no choice. He had to go on.

'Tom!'

He almost jumped out of his skin. He spun around to find her standing there. He couldn't believe she could move so quietly. 'Hi!' he mouthed with much more confidence than he felt.

'Now what?' she whispered.

The light grew worse. Thicker cloud was spreading across the sky. The moon had disappeared. Good. The less visibility there was, the greater their chances of not being seen.

'Ready?' he asked.

They headed cautiously towards the jetty, stopping frequently to listen. A dog started barking. Tom froze. He thought it came from the far side of the village. If so, the dog could not possibly have seen them. But someone else might be out and about! He waited, the hair on his arms bristling. After a long pause, he went forward and knelt down by the side of the fuel store. He looked anxiously up and down the jetty.

The *Ular Ular* was waiting for them. He could hear the creak of her mooring ropes as they strained against the rush of the tide. He turned and whispered in Nancy's ear.

'We'll go on board. You go aft and wait till I tell you to cast off. OK?'

She nodded.

'I'll slip the bow moorings first, to let the tide swing her out. Then she'll be facing downstream. You only cast off when I tell you to. Understand?'

'Got it!' she said. Then added, 'What happens if there's someone sleeping on board?'

Tom gulped. He had not thought of that! Sweat broke out all over his face. Nancy's question had shaken him to the core. 'Then we run like hell back here and pretend to be fast asleep!' He looked around quickly. There was only one way to find out.

'Go!' he urged.

They ran barefooted towards the boat. He saw Nancy scramble on board below the bridge and make her way towards the stern. With his heart thumping like a pile-driver, Tom unhitched the bow rope.

For ten seconds, nothing happened. Then a gap appeared between the bow and the jetty. It grew wider . . . and wider. The bows began to swing out and face downstream. He ran towards the *Ular Ular*'s stern and scrambled on board.

'Wait until she's swung right around,' he told Nancy. 'She's using your rope as a pivot. Now!' he cried. 'Let it go!'

There was a splash as the mooring line fell into the river. The boat hesitated then began to move. The tide bubbled at her bow as the *Ular Ular* slipped away from the jetty, like a thief in the night.

Chapter 37

Duc To held his breath and listened. He put his head on one side, straining to hear the rhythm of the other boy's breathing. With a growing sense of panic he sat up and called, 'Tom? Tom!'

There was no reply.

'Tom?' he cried. 'Where are you?' His words died in the silence. He went to the doorway. It was very dark outside and raining. He shivered in the unexpected cold.

Had they really gone? That idiot, Tom? And Nancy? His Nancy. His only friend. Taken away by this brash newcomer? Duc To's eyes filled with tears. If they had gone, he knew he would never see them again. He didn't give a damn about Tom. But Nancy? He couldn't bear it.

They'd known each other for years. She had been his

best friend. All those confidences and the plans they'd made. And now this! She'd deserted him. It wasn't fair. She had betrayed their friendship. Then a different thought struck him.

Perhaps they hadn't left. Perhaps that clever dick Tom couldn't get the boat started after all! The only way to make sure was to go down to the jetty and see for himself. He still couldn't believe they were trying to steal the *Ular Ular*. It was unthinkable.

There was no point getting his clothes unnecessarily soaked, so he ran naked past the puddles, rubbing at his arms to keep them warm. He reached the jetty and with a sinking heart hurried forward. She was gone! The boat was no longer there! They had taken her! He ran to the far end and looked down at the river. The tide was still flowing out, so they couldn't have left that long ago.

He hopped from one foot to the other, in an agony of indecision. What did he do now? Lin Pao would be incandescent with rage. Duc To thought about this and whimpered. They'd blame him of course. They'd put him in the cage for weeks, months even. They'd say he must have known about it. Days ago. So why hadn't he told them? Even if they believed him about that, they'd still say he could have come to them earlier that night.

And how could he have gone to sleep knowing Tom was planning to steal Lin Pao's boat?

The tears streamed down Duc To's face. Perhaps they'd kill him straight out? Shoot him in the head. Or cut it off! He wailed his misery into the night in long, shuddering sobs that came straight from his broken, frightened heart. Later, he trudged back to his hut, head down like a beaten dog. He got dressed and went to break the news to Lin Pao.

Chapter 38

The tide carried them steadily down river like a piece of driftwood. It was pitch dark. The moon and stars still obscured by heavy cloud.

'Where are we, Tom?' Nancy asked.

He shook his head. 'No idea.'

He stared into the darkness and thought he could make out the loom of a cliff over on the right-hand side. But that was all.

'Why don't you start the engine or switch on the searchlight?' she said.

Tom hesitated. 'I want to. But I don't know how far we are from the village.' He peered down at the river. 'I can't tell how fast we're going.'

'Let's count to a hundred,' she suggested. 'We've got to be clear by then.'

'Make it two hundred. That should be enough. It'll

be really noisy when we start up.'

He wiped the rain from his face. It was getting heavier. He thought of the shoals and the waves awaiting them and gripped the wheel more tightly.

'We'll have to lie up for a bit by those mangroves,' he told her. 'Until there's some daylight. We can't risk going to sea until then.'

Tom was not enjoying this. The initial rush of adrenalin was gone. It had all seemed so simple yesterday. Find the ignition wires, put them together and hey presto! That was it. A ten-second job. What could be easier? But out here, it felt totally different. One slip with the wires and he could fuse every electrical circuit on the boat. And if that happened, they'd just have to sit here and wait for Lin Pao to come and find them.

He licked his lips. 'OK,' he said, hoping he was sounding confident. 'Let's try the engine now. Take this torch. Shine it up under the instrument panel so I can see.'

Nancy knelt on all fours but found she couldn't keep the torch still.

'Lie on your side,' Tom said testily.

She did and that was better.

Tom, meanwhile, lay staring up at the spaghetti of

wiring. His stomach sank. The colours of the thin plastic wires looked quite different in torchlight. He could feel fear gathering between his shoulder blades.

'Can you see them, Tom?' Nancy called, sounding worried. 'They all look the same to me!'

He ignored her. It took an age but finally he found the ignition switch and yanked out one of the wires. He shielded it between the fingers of his left hand. If it touched a patch of bare metal, it would short-circuit everything. With his other hand, he detached the second wire.

He felt sick with apprehension. 'Here goes!'

He touched the two wires together. Nothing happened. He couldn't believe it. To have got this far. The engine coughed. Once, twice, then roared into life. Clouds of exhaust swirled over the stern. Nancy yelled in glee.

They hugged each other and did a little dance across the deck. Tom throttled the engine back and the noise subsided to a powerful beat. He found the searchlight and turned it on. The beam cut through the darkness and played on great patches of jungle on either side.

'Keep your eyes skinned for the mangroves!' he warned. 'We mustn't go past them.' He sat in Lin Pao's chair and breathed more easily. Now they had a fighting chance. He pushed the throttle forward. The propeller started to turn and they moved off under their own power. Away to the east, the first grey of the new dawn was showing.

Chapter 39

Lin Pao heard his name being called. He opened his eyes but remained perfectly still. Had it been a dream? He lay listening. He heard the wind ruffling the palm leaves. A cockerel was crowing, its cry sounding muffled so he knew the weather had turned. At this time of year that meant the monsoon was coming. There'd be a storm later that day.

'Lin Pao. Lin Pao, please wake up.'

It was that boy's voice. Now he could recognize it. He hitched his sarong more tightly around his waist and went out to see Duc To. It was a grey morning. Wisps of mist were gathering in the treetops on the hill opposite. There was more strength in the wind than he had been expecting and he noticed the warning yellow cast of the sky.

The boy flung himself down in front of him.

Lin Pao started back in surprise.

'Get up! Why are you doing that?'

The boy was moaning incoherently. Lin Pao looked at him.

'Duc To,' he cried with a reasonableness he did not feel, 'tell me what's wrong with you. Are you sick?' Then, beginning to understand; 'Something is wrong? What?'

He stooped, seized the boy by the hair and yanked him upright. 'You will tell me, now!' he cried. He listened stony-faced as Duc To began to blurt out the shocking news. When he understood, Lin Pao screamed.

It was an ugly, primeval sound in which fury, disbelief and shock were equally blended. He flung Duc To to the ground and kicked him. Then, he began to run. He raced through the village shouting at them to wake up and to follow. Heads popped out of doorways and men came tumbling out.

He reached the jetty and screamed again. His boat, his beautiful *Ular Ular*, was gone! Taken by children! Livid with rage, he turned and shouted at the village. The pirates were running towards him in alarm, clutching long, curved knives. They came to a ragged halt around him and stood gaping.

Lin Pao shouted at them, 'Duang's boat! Get in it, you fools. They can't have got far!'

Chapter 40

'Hang on tight!' Tom warned. A wave crashed into
them, forcing the bows off to one side. A sheet of spray
slashed at their faces.

'That hurt!' Nancy cried. 'Like it had claws!'

Tom spun the wheel and brought the *Ular Ular* back
on course.

'It'll get worse!' he shouted. 'It's shallow here and the
wind's getting up. See!'

He pointed. Nancy followed his outstretched arm. A
look of horror spread across her face.

'We're not going through that! We can't!'

Ahead of them, the waves were boiling up the sand
into a tossing curtain of brown surf. After the calm of
the river, it was a terrifying sight.

'We've got to,' Tom shouted back. 'It's the way
the ship came. Once we're through, we'll be in

deep water. It'll be easier then.'

'Easier!' she screamed. 'Tom! We can't do it. We'll be drowned! Look at it!'

'We can't go back!' he shouted, suddenly angry with her.

'No! No! No!' she cried. 'Tom. I'm scared! Look at those waves! They're bigger than us!'

'Go down below, if you want. But hurry!'

Nancy shook her head. 'Too late! Look out!'

Close your eyes!' Tom yelled, as a wave picked the *Ular Ular* up and flung her sideways. Tons of water thundered down on top of the boat. The bows disappeared as the sea rose up all around them, wanting to swamp them and drag them under. Nancy's shriek was snatched by the wind and ripped into a thousand pieces. The *Ular Ular* shuddered and slowly began to right herself as water cascaded along her length, back into the sea.

'Hang on!' Tom screamed. This time he could not keep the terror from his own voice. A wall of brown water reared up in front of them. The *Ular Ular*'s bow rose. Her stern fell away as she climbed. In slow motion, Tom watched the wave gather above them in a foaming, hissing overhang. The sky was blotted out. There was a sound like an express train tearing towards them. Tom shut his eyes and prayed. There was a tremendous crash and the next instant they were swooping across its back, the *Ular Ular* rolling and pitching like a bolting horse.

Another wave burst beside them and the bridge was full of water. It surged up and down and tugged at their waists, trying to pull them overboard. Tom fought the wheel until the muscles in his arms and shoulders grew rigid. For a dreadful moment in the middle of it all, he thought the engine had stalled.

He was aware of Nancy huddled up beside him. She was wedged in between the captain's chair and the front of the bridge. She stared at him with huge, brown eyes. He gave her a nod and tried to smile. She was alive and still there, thank God.

Hours later it seemed they were over the worst. The height of the waves dropped and their steep-sided ferocity eased. It was still rough, with a lumpy sea running and the occasional wave bursting over their bows.

Tom bent over her. 'We're through,' he told her. 'It's going to be all right. You see!'

She pushed herself upright and looked around. 'All that surf's gone. You were right!'

He saw she was shaking. 'Have a look in the cabin.

There may be dry clothes in one of the lockers.'

She nodded and looked around the bridge. 'Where's all the water gone?'

'Self-bailing,' Tom told her. 'She's got an automatic pump that chucks it over the side. This boat's got everything.' He patted the wheel almost affectionately. 'How you feeling?' he asked her.

She gave a lopsided grin. 'I survived.' Her smiled broadened. 'Tom, you were brilliant.'

He shrugged. 'So brilliant, I left the chart out. Now it's blown away.'

Nancy looked worried. 'Do you know where we are?'

'Sort of.'

Nancy thought about this. 'So where we heading?'

He pointed to the compass. 'It's basic navigation. We're going due east. Towards Malaysia. We can't miss it.'

'How far?' she asked.

He tried to sound relaxed. 'A hundred miles. Maybe ninety. Depends where we come ashore.'

She, shook her head. 'I don't even want to think about it. I'm going to put a kettle on. If it's not been smashed.'

After she had gone below, Tom dropped their speed and found the boat rode the waves with an easier motion. Every now and then, he stood on tiptoe scanning the water ahead for any sign of shoals or breaking water. He looked back at the headland above the mangrove trees. And remembered the pirates!

He wondered if a pursuing boat could see them this far out? He checked again, feeling suddenly anxious. Lin Pao must know by now what had happened. Should he crack on speed again? He blinked. Something odd was happening. The headland was not as clear as it had been a minute ago. Five minutes later, it had disappeared altogether and he realized that fog or rain, or a combination of both, was rolling towards them.

Now what? Should he keep heading into the Straits? Or wait until he could see where they were going? Nancy came up on deck carefully balancing two mugs of tea. It was hot and sweet and made with powdered milk. Nothing had ever tasted so good.

'Brilliant!' he told her.

'Tom, it's getting really foggy,' she told him. 'Shouldn't we slow down or put the radar on?'

He made a face. 'Radar's not much use in very bad weather,' he explained. 'It can't penetrate heavy rain. The screen gets all fuzzy. Besides, this one's broken.'

'Tom,' she said, pointing to the sea. 'It's getting smaller and smaller out there.

Everything's closing in.'

Nancy was right. A few minutes later, they were plunged into a world of grey half-light and lashing rain.

Chapter 41

Lin Pao hung on to the side of the bridge as the boat crashed through the waves. The deck was awash with water. Given the conditions, he was driving her recklessly.

Like a ruddy speedboat, Chou thought then shouted, 'We're about three miles out. Can't see very much.'

Lin Pao heard the rebuke in his voice. The man was right. It was time to get his feelings back under control and start a proper search for the *Ular Ular*. Finding her was the only thing that mattered.

'Ease speed!' he ordered.

The pirates looked at one another and nodded in relief. Chou went up into the bows and the rest of the crew spread out along the sides.

Lin Pao studied the chart and plotted the search pattern. He drew a five-mile-long square on the chart.

They would travel up and down a couple of times inside the square, then move on another five miles and begin all over again. He looked behind him and saw the line of heavy rain approaching.

Lin Pao cursed. Those damn children might still get away with it. He snatched another glance over his shoulder and saw the rain was appreciably nearer. Damn them!

'Five hundred dollars for the first man to spot her!' he shouted. The pirates gave a shout then looked unhappily at the approaching storm. They knew what was coming.

Lin Pao heard the *bleep-bleep* of the ship-to-shore telephone. He ducked down below the windscreen to hear better and clamped a hand to the headpiece. The Dragon Lady's voice cut through the background static like a steel blade.

'I've just been told what's happened,' she said. 'The Lee boy and that wicked, wicked girl. She's the dangerous one! She was listening to us last night, and before, probably. She knows everything!'

Lin Pao took a deep breath and strained to hear.

Her voice shook. 'If they get away, she will betray us. Do you understand what I'm saying, Lin Pao? She will ruin everything! So find them, Lin Pao. Find them!'

* * *

The telephone clicked off and Lin Pao let his breath out in a long, loud sigh. He stood up and looked quickly around. He saw grey waves under a sullen sky and a horizon closing in on them. The words 'Mission Impossible' flashed through his mind. And at that precise moment, the man at the wheel beside him let out a yell and pointed. Less than a mile away, a shaft of light pierced the murk. The pirates had a brief, tantalizing glimpse of the *Ular Ular*.

Even as Lin Pao screamed the order, Chou opened up with the machine gun. The stink of cordite came whipping aft as the gun fired a long burst. Bright red flashes arched towards the target. Brass shell cases clattered on to the deck. Lin Pao seized the wheel and threw the throttle wide open.

The boat came around in a tight, slipping circle, heeling sharply to one side and smacking into the waves with a noise like cannon fire. When he straightened her, there was no sign of the *Ular Ular*. Instead, long fingers of fog began fluttering towards them. Soon, they were wrapping themselves around the boat. Lin Pao cursed his fate but he was not going to lose his beloved *Ular* now. He drove straight for her last sighting.

Streaming with water, the boat settled her stern deeper into the sea and gathered herself for the chase.

Chapter 42

From the corner of his eye, Tom saw the row of red flashes stretching towards him. He had a brief glimpse of the black-sided pirate boat before a bank of fog swirled between them.

He reacted instinctively and swung the wheel hard over in a 180-degree turn.

'Hang on, Nancy!' he shouted.

The *Ular Ular* came round very quickly. He watched the compass needle swing madly then settle on to the new course.

Nancy was shouting at him from the cabin. 'Are we OK? What's happening?'

'We're OK,' he told her, which was a lie. How big a lie, they'd both know soon enough. His instincts told him that the pirates would expect him to have panicked and to be making a dash for it on his previous heading. By going this way, he was turning back towards the shore and sailing deeper into the fog. And that was what he was banking on!

He waited a little while longer then brought the boat to a standstill. He kept the engine just ticking over.

'What are you doing?' cried Nancy, by now thoroughly alarmed.

Tom put a finger to his lips. 'It's them!' he warned. 'It must be Lin Pao. He saw us back there but I think we've given him the slip.'

She looked horrified and opened her mouth wide.

He seized her by the arm and shook her firmly. 'Don't make any noise. Just listen out for them!'

They drifted in silence for what seemed an age. Now that they were no longer underway, the *Ular Ular* rolled uncomfortably.

'What about the engine?' Nancy asked in a low voice. 'Can't you switch it off? Only the exhaust's getting really bad.'

Tom shook his head. 'I can't risk trying to start it again. It's too rough!'

Later, she put a hand to her mouth and swallowed several times. She made being sick signs. Tom pointed vigorously to the cabin down below.

'They might hear you up here!'

She leant over the side and splashed seawater over her face. 'I'll be all right,' she told him and managed a reluctant grin.

Tom was just congratulating himself on having outwitted the pirates when they heard the steady throb of an engine approaching. They stood transfixed with horror, staring into the impenetrable gloom, while it grew louder. Soon, they were surrounded by the noise. The fog played with the sound like a distorting mirror in a fairground. It was everywhere. Sometimes loud; other times, fading. But it never seemed to go away. It was always there. And all they could do was to stand shivering, waiting for the pirate boat to loom out of the murk and catch them.

And then, the engine was switched off. Nancy squeezed Tom's hand so hard he almost yelled out loud. They stared into the eerie, swirling world until their eyes watered and they had lost all sense of direction.

'What about our engine?' Nancy whispered. 'They'll hear it!'

Tom did not move. Could not move. He was beaten. He did not know what to do. That was the moment when they heard Chou's voice. It was so close they flinched away and almost tripped over each other. Nancy bit her fingers to stop herself crying out loud.

The hairs stood up on Tom's neck.

'I'll use that Duc To as shark bait when we get back,' Chou told someone. 'I'll gut him myself. Just you wait.'

'And those other ones,' another voice agreed. 'They deserve everything that's coming.' Then his voice faded.

Soon afterwards the engine started up, and a minute later its wake slapped against the *Ular Ular*'s hull. It began to rain, heavily again. Soon it was torrential.

A grim-faced Tom said, 'Let's get out of here!'

Nancy put her face in her hands and wept.

Chapter 43

Lin Pao looked at his watch.

Chou saw him doing this and grumbled, 'We've been out here three hours now and no sign of them anywhere!' He spat over the side. 'It's this ruddy weather. Any other day and we'd have got 'em. Easy!'

Lin Pao wiped the rain from his face and said nothing.

'We've tried everything,' Chou went on. 'Every trick in the book. We've doubled back, circled, criss-crossed and listened. For nothing!' He put a fresh matchstick in the corner of his mouth and chewed viciously. 'Perhaps they've rolled her over!'

Lin Pao stiffened in horror. For a moment he imagined the *Ular Ular* lying on the sea floor in sixty metres of water.

'Mark you! We've not seen any oil or wreckage,' Chou added hurriedly.

Lin Pao did not reply. For once in his life he felt totally beaten. How could he have lost the *Ular Ular* when she had been so close? Not to mention those damn children. But he had. He glared around the bridge in disgust. It was filthy. The entire boat was filthy. Duang might have had big ship experience but he was not a good boat skipper.

The fuel gauge did not seem to be working properly. He tapped the glass. It flickered. He tapped it again, harder this time.

'It's empty!' he gasped.

'We've not been out long enough!' cried Chou. 'It's impossible!'

But as they looked around at the dirt and grime, they both knew it wasn't. They stared at each other in horror. Chou beat his head with his fists.

'Isn't there someone from Duang's crew on board now?' Lin Pao asked.

Chou nodded. 'He was too sick to go on the ship with the others.'

'Bring him!'

When the man was dragged in front of him, Lin Pao pulled out his pistol and put it to the man's head.

'Tell me, you slab-faced piece of carrion,' he began, 'was this boat properly refuelled after your last mission?'

The pirate began to shake. 'No, sir! No, Mr Lin Pao, sir! Duang said we'd do it the next day. But by then we were all busy painting the ship, Forgive me, sir!'

Lin Pao kicked the man on the kneecap. 'Get rid of him.'

'Over the side?' Chou asked.

Lin Pao shook his head. 'It wasn't his fault.' Then, to the man at the wheel, 'Turn her around. We're going back to base.'

This is the end, he thought as the men left the bridge. How can you run anything properly if the people you trust can't even be bothered to get the basics right?

His dislike of Duang was turning to hatred. The boats were kept fully refuelled at all times in case they had to put to sea in a hurry. Or even, fight their way out. Duang knew this perfectly well. It was the most important commandment the pirates had.

But, he told himself bitterly, he was also at fault. He had not checked the fuel level before they left, that dawn. It had never occurred to him.

Lin Pao hunched his shoulders into his jacket and stood bareheaded in the rain. If it wasn't all so unfair, it might even be hilarious. As things now stood, Duang was the pirate captain who would be remembered for years to come as the one who brought a ship and a cargo worth a fortune safely into port. He would be praised and honoured. There would be songs about him.

By contrast, he, Lin Pao, would be a laughing-stock. A joke pirate. Children had stolen his boat. They had outwitted him and escaped. And now he was returning to his base like a cringing dog because he had run out of fuel.

He was mortified.

A little later, he realized that he must radio the Dragon Lady and give her the news. He sat upright in his bridge chair, his face set in an expressionless mask, while the crew looked uncomfortable and incredulous, by turn. The man at the wheel was careful not to meet his eye.

They motored past the mangroves, along the river by the cliffs, and saw the village lying ahead. As they approached the jetty, Lin Pao's heart sank still further. She was waiting for him there.

He could not meet her gaze.

'Where are they?' she asked.

He tried to explain. 'There was fog. Duang's boat was not refuelled . . .' His voice trailed away.

'You are a fool. But Duang is the bigger one!'

'There was a gale at first. Then, bad fog,' he told her wearily. 'They must have capsized or been run down.' He spread his hands, willing her to believe him.

'But we can't be sure. Can we, Lin Pao? We can take nothing for granted.' She rapped her stick on the wooden planks. 'We will have to leave here. There is another place I know, where we will be welcomed.'

He looked at her horrified. 'Leave here!'

She glared at him. 'You have become a parrot, Lin Pao. Yes! Leave! Now I must tell the Family. Help me up to the house.' She took his arm.

'It's not all your fault, Lin Pao,' she told him, when she next stopped to get her breath. 'That wicked minx, Nancy, was entirely my responsibility. She must have been listening and spying on me for years. And as for Captain Lee's brat, I should have kept him in the cage until it was all over.'

Patiently, Lin Pao helped her to the top of the steps. 'The local people were good to us,' she told him. 'I don't want them to suffer if the military come. So put this crew of yours to work, Lin Pao. They've got twenty-four hours to refuel, load ammunition, food, water and destroy the huts. We must be well away by this time tomorrow.'

Chapter 44

Captain Lee breathed a sigh of relief and looked up from the radar screen. 'That's the worst over,' he called across to Duang. 'We're well past Singapore now.' He indicated the row of lights twinkling along the horizon. 'That's the east coast of Malaysia over there. We'll be in open water in an hour's time.'

Duang cracked open a pistachio nut. There was a small pile of shells under his chair. He did not look around. 'How long before we get to Ping Lo?' he grunted.

'At this speed?' Captain Lee walked across to the chart table and considered. 'Seventy-two hours, maybe more if that main bearing gets any worse.' He frowned at Duang's impassive back. 'I don't think you appreciate what a good job my engineers are doing down there!'

Duang said nothing.

'Look!' Captain Lee snapped. 'I want to get to Ping Lo every bit as much as you! I want to see my son and my wife again. Don't you forget that!'

Duang cracked another nut. 'You might be happy to get there, Captain,' he said slowly. 'But I know your engineers aren't. The Chinese will hang on to them until your shipping company pays to get them back. Two months in a Chinese jail isn't much fun. Take my word for it!'

Captain Lee's voice rose. 'And I tell you, they've worked wonders! What do you know about ships like this?' and he swore under his breath.

Duang swung around in his chair. 'So it's thanks to them, we've got to crawl along at this speed, is it? Is that what you're telling me?' He spat on the deck. 'Maybe if I threw them overboard, one at a time, things might get better!'

Captain Lee shook his head in despair. They had had this conversation before. 'I need some sleep,' he told Duang. 'Let me have a couple of hours. There's no ship within ten miles of us out here. Keep to this course and you'll be fine.'

Duang nodded. 'Sleep as long as you want, Captain.' He jerked a thumb at one of the pirates standing at the back of the bridge. 'Go with him,' he ordered. 'Don't let him out of your sight for a moment.'

The pirate unslung his rifle and prodded Captain Lee in the back with it.

'Sweet dreams!' Duang called after them.

After the two men had left the bridge, Duang padded across to the radar. He spent a couple of minutes studying it. He also glanced at the ship's safe and thought about the ten thousand dollars stacked neatly inside. He licked his lips. On impulse, he left the bridge and began the long descent to the engine room. The temperature down there was a good ten degrees hotter than on deck. A solitary pirate got to his feet as Duang entered. A rifle lay beside him on the catwalk.

Duang paused to get his breath. He looked down on to the gleaming, throbbing heart of the ship and the handful of men in overalls fussing over it. The place smelt of hot oil and stale electricity.

'Come with me!' Duang barked at the pirate.

The chief engineer was red-eyed with fatigue. He took Duang to look at the huge stainless steel propeller shaft that rumbled and rotated under the arc lights. He showed him the damaged bearing. Duang shrugged. There was not much to see.

They knelt on the hard steel deck at the entrance to

the shaft and looked along its length. At the far end was the ship's propeller itself. Every revolution it made was driving the ship closer to Ping Lo and the bonanza awaiting them. Duang watched it rotate. It seemed to be running smoothly enough. An engineer pushed past them and started pouring oil on to it.

'Stops the bearing seizing up,' the chief engineer shouted in his ear.

How convenient, Duang thought, to have the man appearing with his oil can like that. He was sure now. Certain. They were trying to take him for a fool! He got to his feet.

'Crank it up!' he shouted. 'You can fool your skipper all you want. But you don't fool me. I want full speed! Now!'

The chief engineer started towards him, his hands reaching out to shake Duang. 'You're mad! You're crazy mad!'

Duang's bodyguard cocked his rifle and jammed the muzzle into the engineer's stomach.

'I said full speed ahead!' Duang roared. 'Get on with it!'

Chapter 45

'When's this horrible fog going to lift?' Nancy cried angrily. 'I'm sick of it.'

Tom bent over the compass and checked their heading for the third time that minute. They were making a steady ten knots. The sea had fallen dramatically and only the occasional wave now burst over the bows.

'You're sure we've not been going around in circles?' she demanded, sounding petulant. 'I mean, we wouldn't know, would we? Not in all this fog and stuff. We could be going in circles or heading back towards the village!'

Tom shook his head. 'No way! It might seem like that, but it's not true. We've been heading due east for hours.' He pointed to the compass. 'That's how I know. We're miles away. They won't catch us now.'

'So where are we?' she demanded.

He hesitated. 'Getting near the coast of Malaysia.'

She shivered and began hugging herself. 'Shouldn't we be slowing down? We don't want to hit rocks or the shore or something. Why can't this fog just go?'

'It saved us back there. I'm not complaining,' Tom reminded her. 'I just wish the radar was working, then we could see how close we were getting.'

Nancy put a hand on his arm. 'Listen!'

'What is it?'

She waved him to silence. Ten seconds crawled past.

'Nancy! What is it? Tell me! It's not surf, is it?'

'Slow down! Right down!'

Tom did so and waited, listening hard. He looked up and for a fleeting moment saw a patch of blue sky, high above them. The fog shifted and it disappeared.

'Nancy!' he called, almost laughing with relief. 'The fog's lifting. I can see the sky!'

'Shut up!' she shouted, furious with him. She thrust out an arm. 'There's something out there. Can't you hear it? Something ahead of us.' She waited a moment longer then said, 'I can feel it coming!'

And at that moment, he heard it too. It was a sound like waves tumbling and crashing. Tom's heart raced. There must be a reef ahead. Dead ahead! He gripped the wheel and put it hard over. Nancy screamed in his ear as a towering black wall loomed up and they saw the great bows of a ship slicing towards them!

He had a fleeting glimpse of a huge anchor with water dripping from it. Then he was wrestling with the wheel as they went bucketing down the ship's side. White water crashed down on the *Ular Ular*'s deck. He saw rusted steel plates and the green glow of a navigation light far above his head. A row of portholes gleamed yellow and were gone. They both heard the rhythmical *slap-slap* of the propeller growing louder and knew there was nothing they could do to avoid it.

He was aware of Nancy's arms around him as the stern closed in above them. He saw the massive rudder post thick with barnacles in front of them. A wave exploded beside the boat, flinging the *Ular Ular* a crucial metre away from the hull. The thump of the propeller was deafening. They swept past the nearest blade and fell sideways, into the deep trench of the ship's wake, like a stick going over a waterfall.

The *Ular Ular* staggered as a wall of water met her head on. Waves swept across her deck and exploded against the bridge in ragged crests. She reared up, shaking from bow to stern, fighting for life while the sea pounded her thin steel sides.

The waves swept Tom and Nancy off their feet and rolled them over and over like pieces of driftwood. For a terrifying moment, Tom knew he had been swept overboard. He was in the sea looking down at the *Ular Ular*. The next wave flung him back on the bridge. Sometime later, he was aware of Nancy shouting at him from the cabin stairway. Then a fresh wave washed over him and he was struggling for breath again.

When at long last the *Ular Ular* came upright, draining seawater like a rock at half-tide, they were both still there. Half drowned, barely aware of what was happening around them, yet somehow hanging on to life.

The boat wallowed sluggishly, her engine swamped and fifty centimetres of water surging freely in the cabin. How long they lay there, they had no idea. They had no sense of time passing. When they eventually realized the *Ular Ular* was not going to sink, they huddled together inside the battered bridge and fell into an exhausted sleep.

The sun woke them. The sun and the sound of shouting from the crews of two fishing boats. One of them came alongside, its nets piled in untidy heaps and a curious crew staring at them. Willing hands helped them on board.

'Where are we?' Tom asked.

'Fourteen miles from Kola village,' an elderly man told him. 'Is this your boat?'

'Don't tell them too much,' Nancy murmured. 'Just in case.'

Tom shivered. Just in case they take us back, he thought.

The fisherman's voice rose. 'This your boat?'

Tom hopped from one foot to the other. 'Sort of,' he lied awkwardly. 'It's my father's, only we got separated in all that fog.'

The fisherman stared at him open-mouthed and pointed to the machine gun. 'What sort of work does your father do?'

'He's in the police,' Nancy chipped in. 'It's an anti-pirate patrol boat. He was showing it to us.'

'There were two boats,' Tom added. 'Only we got split up.'

The fishermen frowned.

'There'll be a big reward for rescuing it,' Nancy told him.

The rest of the crew gave a cheer and began to laugh and whoop amongst themselves.

'Sounds good to me!' said the elderly man. He shouted across to the other boat then said, 'I'll take you ashore now.'

He took them in a wide circle around the *Ular Ular*. As they watched, they saw the other fishing boat start to take her in tow.

'Can you save her?' Tom asked.

The elderly man nodded. 'She's well built and the weather's improving. She'll be all right. But how about the two of you? We've a medical centre in our village and a police post a mile further on,' he told them.

'Police first,' said Tom. 'I've got to tell my father what's happened.'

The fisherman nodded. 'I'll take you there myself.'

Chapter 46

The lights were burning late in the Commissioner's office. The Special Branch man stifled a yawn and sneaked a glance at his watch.

'It's all gone quiet,' the Commissioner was complaining. 'No signal traffic from the pirates, no faxes. Patou's not been doing anything. Nothing yet from the navy or air force. And all the time, this ship is slipping through our fingers.'

He thrust back his chair and began to pace up and down. 'What on earth am I going to tell the minister?'

No one said anything. The Commissioner scowled at them. 'Well?' he challenged. 'None of you got any ideas? You're the so-called experts.'

There was a knock and an orderly put his head around the door.

'There's an urgent call for Sergeant Chung from the Kola police post!'

'Where the hell's that?' the Commissioner barked.

'West coast of Malaysia,' the Special Branch man told him. 'Halfway up.'

'They've got a boy there name of Lee. Tom Lee. Do I put it through?'

There was a shout of excitement. They crowded around Sergeant Chung, bending their heads towards the telephone he was holding. He waved them to silence, then turned his back when the call came through.

'Tom?' He put up his thumb in triumph. When he had finished, he replaced the receiver and, with a voice thick with emotion, cried:

'She's called the *Azura* and she left two days ago for Ping Lo!'

Chapter 47

Something was wrong. Captain Lee swung his legs off the bunk and stood in his bare feet on the cabin floor. The ship was not underway! There were no vibrations underfoot. He crossed to the door of the cabin and flicked on the light switch. Only the dim emergency lighting came on.

Oh my God! he thought. What's happened? What have they done?

The door was locked. He pounded at it with his fist and started to shout. No one came. He ducked over to the porthole and peered out. It was still very dark. He thought it was an hour or so before dawn. There was a ship out there. He could see its lights. He gasped as a dreadful thought occurred to him. Would Duang have had the sense to turn on the emergency navigation lights to warn other ships to keep clear? Did he even know about them?

Or was there some huge, unstoppable oil tanker, even now bearing down on them? And was he about to be drowned like a rat in his own cabin! Frantic now at the thought, he pummelled the door.

There were voices outside. A key rattled in the lock. Two armed pirates stood there. 'Come with us! Move,' one of them ordered.

'Where's Duang?' he yelled. 'What's happening? I must check the radar!' He strode past them, shrugging off a restraining arm. He heard a gun being cocked but ignored it. The bridge was empty. A quick scan of the radar showed they were in no immediate danger. The nearest ship was ten miles away on a safe heading. There was no sign of land on the screen. That meant they were well out into the South China Sea.

He knew then what had happened. That fool Duang must have increased speed dramatically. And now the bearing had gone. He switched on the emergency navigation lights and let them hurry him down to the engine room.

The heat in there was overpowering. In the dim emergency lighting, men's bodies glistened with sweat. Their shadows flickered across the outcrops of machinery and their upraised voices were quickly swallowed in that huge space. The stench of boiling oil and burnt out machinery was everywhere. It hung like a shroud over the silent engine and the seized propeller shaft. Duang and the chief engineer stood facing each other. The pirate was screaming abuse.

A blind rage seized Captain Lee. He started running along the steel catwalk, sliding down ladders four steps at a time, on to the engine room floor. There was only one man to blame for this. One stupid, idiotic man who had now put Tom's life and everyone else's in even greater danger.

'Duang!' he roared at the top of his voice, thrusting his way through the pirates. 'You great fool! What have you done?'

Duang put his hands on his hips and shook his head furiously. 'Sabotage!' he screamed. 'They sabotaged it!'

Captain Lee stood facing him. 'Sabotage? Rubbish! You're the one who's broken my ship! You're the fool! And you've put my son's life in danger. You're an idiot!'

Duang's eyes bulged. His hand went to his belt and the knife he carried. As he did so, a pirate with a rifle pushed in between them and forced Captain Lee back.

'Leave it, Skipper!' the chief engineer warned, grabbing his arm and pulling him further away. 'Or you'll get yourself killed! There's nothing any of us can do now. The shaft's seized solid. We'll need a tow.'

'Hear that, Duang?' Captain Lee shouted, still shaking with fury. 'You're going to need a tug. Better tell your bosses to get one organized. Fast!' He tapped the side of his head and laughed at the expression on Duang's face. 'You've really blown it! Haven't you? I'm glad I'm not in your shoes!'

Duang looked at him for a very long time. Silently, he turned and walked away. Most of the pirates followed. A door clanged shut behind them.

'What do you mean, "in his shoes"?' the chief engineer said dryly. 'It's not much fun being in ours, come to that.'

Chapter 48

Mr Patou was opening the morning post. He was smiling. An unexpected cheque had arrived and he was trying to decide whether to bank it this morning or leave it until after lunch. It was a pleasant enough dilemma. Outside his door, the workshop was humming. The customer this time was an Australian department store.

The telephone rang. The familiar, harsh voice said, 'We must meet. Immediately. At your place.'

Mr Patou frowned. This was a dramatic departure from normal. He shrugged. 'Fine by me. Later today?'

'Now!' And the line went dead.

Ten minutes later, Mr Patou stood up with a welcoming smile as the man came in. The smile was entirely for his secretary's benefit.

'Close the door, tight!' he called after her. He

started to say, 'This is an unexpected pleasure,' when the man interrupted.

'No pleasure! We've got trouble. Two lots of big trouble!'

Mr Patou gaped.

The man looked around the office. 'I want your code books and all fax copies. Everything. Get them now.'

Mr Patou sat up in a hurry. 'Why? What's happened?'

The man scowled. 'No incriminating evidence. We need to put your papers in very safe place.'

'Evidence?' Mr Patou gasped. 'What are you talking about?' A nasty thought struck him. Evidence usually meant the police. 'What's happening?' he insisted. 'I've a right to know.'

The man hesitated. 'Some people have stolen a boat and escaped from our village. They know too much. Better for us to be safe.'

'Who are these "people",' Mr Patou demanded. 'Do you mean pirates? Your own people?'

The man looked embarrassed. He shifted in his chair and looked at the floor. Mr Patou had never seen him behave like this before. His alarm grew.

The man cleared his throat. 'One of them is the son of ship's captain. Tom Lee.'

Mr Patou glared at him in disbelief. 'A child! You let a child get away. With a boat!'

The man shook his head. 'We think he's dead. Drowned.'

'But you can't take the chance, is that it?'

The man nodded.

Mr Patou got to his feet and went across to the big safe. 'Did you bring a bag with you?'

Carefully, he went through the contents of the safe. 'That's everything,' he said five minutes later. 'So tell me what do I do now? What's happening to me?'

The man stuffed the last of the files into a plastic carrier bag. 'You sit tight,' he said. 'No one knows about you. We will contact you when this is all over.'

Mr Patou thought quickly. He wondered if it was an omen. A heaven-sent opportunity to get out with his skin still intact. A chance to retire, even? There was something else the man had said.

'You told me there were two lots of trouble. What's the other?'

This touched a nerve in the triad. He suddenly banged his fist down on Mr Patou's desk. 'The ship has broken down! Now we have to find a tug!'

Mr Patou put his hands on his head and stared at him. 'I don't believe it!'

The man scowled. 'We think the crew has done sabotage. But we cannot be sure.'

'So where is she?'

'A hundred miles east of Singapore.' He wagged a finger at Mr Patou. 'But you must tell no one. The Family are very angry. I have not told you about this. Understand? Or else . . .' He left the threat hanging in the air between them.

Mr Patou made himself smile as the man left, in case any of his staff were watching. Then he collapsed into his chair, his brain in a whirl. His world was collapsing.

On the other side of the city, two of the men on duty at the Special Monitoring Unit took their headphones off and grinned at each other. The bug in Mr Patou's office was working perfectly. They had heard every word. 'You tell Sergeant Chung right away,' the shorter of them said. 'And I'll pass it on to the Commissioner's office. Looks like they all owe us one. A very big one!'

Chapter 49

It was noisy inside the helicopter. Sergeant Chung had flown up at daybreak to meet Tom and Nancy at the Kola police post. Now, two hours after their leaving the little place with its corrugated-iron roof and flagpole, they were approaching Singapore.

It was the first time either of them had been in a helicopter and they had spent the journey with their noses pressed to the Perspex windows. As the helicopter banked, they caught their first glimpse of the island from the air. Tom and Nancy stared down in amazement at the skyscrapers. There were literally hundreds of them, scattered like mushrooms everywhere they looked. Outside the harbour, a huge armada of ships lay at anchor, awaiting their turn to collect or discharge cargo.

Sergeant Chung's voice rasped in their headphones.

'We'll be landing at police headquarters in three minutes. And Tom! Your mother's already there with Mrs Chung. But remember, we can only let you have twenty minutes with her. Then, we must finish debriefing you both. There've been developments. Big developments,' he added.

'What sort of developments?' Nancy asked. But Sergeant Chung was already talking to someone else.

The engine note changed as the helicopter slowed. Seconds later, they were hovering over a concrete landing pad, at the foot of a tower block. A small figure, a little apart from the others, was waving frantically as they landed. She had a handkerchief in one hand and a large handbag in the other.

'Mum!' Tom shouted and ducked under the swishing rotor blades. He ran towards her, his heart singing. Moments later, he was swinging her off her feet and hugging her. Mrs Lee alternately laughed and sobbed.

'They'll find him, Tom,' she cried breathlessly. 'They'll find him. They know where to look. Thanks to you!' A little later, she blew her nose loudly into her handkerchief and it was Mrs Chung's turn to congratulate him. Tom felt odd seeing her again. The last time they had met, his father had been there. Tom could remember everything they had talked about. Now, he didn't quite know what to say.

He guessed the other people around them were police. He noticed their set expressions and felt a distinct pang of unease. Was there a problem he didn't know about? Would he really see his father again? Angrily, he dismissed the thought as defeatist. After all, if he had been able to get this far on his own, surely they had to succeed with all their resources?

He watched his mother take Nancy under her wing. 'You've been so brave!' she was saying. 'I don't know anyone who could have done all that!'

'Well,' said Nancy, with a smile. 'There's Tom for one.'

Moments later, they were whisked away to the Commissioner's office. After the official introductions and congratulations, it was time to get down to business. The Commissioner brought them all up to date.

'Thanks to Tom and Nancy here,' he began, 'we know the *Serota Star* is now sailing as the *Azura*. She's heading for Ping Lo in China with a crew of pirates on board. Captain Lee and his crew are being held hostage.' He paused and looked directly at Tom and Nancy.

'Thanks to some good work by our Special Monitoring Unit, we've learnt a good deal more in the past couple of hours.' And he brought them both up to date with what had happened earlier that morning in Mr Patou's office.

'Now,' he went on. 'You might think that all we have to do is to find the *Azura* and that's that. It sounds straightforward enough. But it isn't quite so easy.' He shook his head. 'The sea is a big place. A very big place with hundred of ships on it.' He hesitated and looked grave.

'We also have to ask ourselves what will be the pirates' reaction when we do find her? What about the hostages? There are twelve members of Captain Lee's crew on board that ship. And I've no doubt that their lives are more in danger now than at any other time. The ship is drifting. The pirates are waiting to find out what's happening next. They'll be getting more and more stressed.'

Tom's mouth was suddenly dry. He felt Nancy grip his arm.

The Commissioner continued, 'The pirates have two choices. They can hire a tug and be towed all the way to China. But if they do that, they'll be worried that the authorities might become suspicious and investigate. After all, there's a repair yard right here in Singapore. Their other choice is to cut their losses and abandon the ship.'

He looked around the room. 'And if that happens, I don't hold out much hope for any of the hostages!'

There was a long silence. 'I've already told the air force not to fly too low, or more than once, over any ship. It's going to make their job much more difficult to find the target. But we must do everything we can not to alert the pirates. It's going to be very difficult.'

Tom frowned. The Commissioner had used the word 'target'. Why did that set his mind racing? Hadn't the *Serota Star* had been targeted before? And he was back on the *Ular Ular*'s bridge again. Looking at a large dial with some numbers scrawled across it. Of course! The Radio Direction Finder.

He nudged Sergeant Chung. 'I think I know how to find her.'

'What?' gasped Sergeant Chung. 'How?'

Tom was sure now. 'It's called a Radio Direction Finder. There was a receiver in Lin Pao's boat. I'm certain the pirates bugged my dad's ship when it was in Singapore. That's how they found him that night. The wavelength is eighty-eight point one.'

Sergeant Chung's eyes widened. 'You're sure?'

Tom nodded.

'Excuse me, sir!' Sergeant Chung called, suddenly standing up. 'But I think Tom may have the answer to that problem!'

Chapter 50

Lin Pao slowly climbed the hundred steps to the Dragon Lady's house. Halfway there, he stopped to mop his brow. The fog and cold of yesterday's storm was already a memory. Today was hot and humid, with the afternoon sun scorching down. He wondered if this was the last time he'd be doing this. At the seventy-seventh step he paused and thought about Duang.

By Lin Pao's reckoning, the *Azura* should be approaching Ping Lo. She might even be there. He imagined the happy scene: the congratulations and the praise heaped on Duang. His hatred of the man flared up again. He climbed the remaining steps quickly, unable to hide his resentment.

She was waiting for him in her usual high-backed chair. She sat ramrod-straight, her gnarled hands clasped together on top of her stick. A small wooden

244

chest lay on the floor nearby. Lin Pao guessed it contained her jewellery.

He bowed his head. 'We are ready for sea.'

'Do I need to check the fuel stocks?' she asked acidly.

Lin Pao said nothing but her words cut him to the quick. From now on, no matter how long his life, he knew that this was how he would always be remembered.

The Dragon Lady was studying him, watching to see his reaction. 'Well, if it's any consolation, that fool Duang seems to have ruined everything else.'

Lin Pao did not say anything but his heart leapt.

Her eyes held his. 'The ship's broken down the other side of Singapore. Do you remember they told us she had a worn bearing?'

He nodded, biting his tongue to stop himself calling out.

'It's my guess,' she went on, 'Duang either forgot about it or ignored it and drove the ship too hard.'

With an extraordinary effort of will, Lin Pao kept his face expressionless. But inside his heart was pounding. 'So what will happen now?'

She shook her head. 'The Family are chartering a tug but it's not available until midnight tonight. It'll be with him early tomorrow morning. But you see the

245

danger, don't you, Lin Pao?'

He thought for a moment. 'Meaning it's a long tow to Ping Lo?'

She nodded and gave him a rare smile. 'Aren't you glad it's not your problem?'

He didn't know what to say and so said nothing.

She studied him critically. 'Your pocket's torn. Standards must be slipping.'

His hand went straight to the rip in his jacket He had made it that morning while looking for the boy, Duc To. 'I'll darn it tonight,' he told her.

The Dragon Lady shook her head. 'For heaven's sake get one of the village women to do it for you!'

Lin Pao did not reply.

'Very well,' she said getting to her feet. 'You've come for your orders. We leave tomorrow at dawn. Chou will collect me and bring me to the boat.'

He watched her go. Then he bowed and went out rejoicing into the sunlight.

Chapter 51

The sunset was staining the sea blood-red. Along the eastern horizon, a line of thunderclouds was massing over the South China Sea. To the west, the crew of the air force plane could follow the mountain range that formed the spine of Malaysia. At three thousand metres, they could see sixty miles in all directions. Their patrol had been scrambled hours ago to look for the *Azura*. Just before take-off, they had been joined by a tall police technician who sat beside the pilot monitoring an RDF receiver.

'It'll be dark in twenty minutes,' the pilot warned him over the intercom.

'Can we do one more sweep then?' he asked, hardly bothering to look up from his machine.

The pilot breathed hard then nodded. It would after all be the last one they'd make that day. He looked at his radar display. There were two ships about twenty miles ahead. Both were on similar courses and probably heading for China. From this distance and height, the plane was well below their horizon.

'They're three or four miles apart,' he told the technician. 'So I'll fly up the middle. Can you wiggle your box of tricks at them?'

The technician frowned. 'No,' he said. 'I told you. It doesn't work like that. I need a clear line of sight. Can't we just get behind each boat in turn so I can track 'em properly?'

The pilot frowned. 'My orders are not to make it look obvious. It's got to seem like a casual overfly.'

The technician said nothing.

The pilot looked down at the gathering dusk. The horizon was shrinking fast as night closed in. It would be even gloomier at sea level. An aircraft would be very hard to spot from the deck of a ship in conditions like these. He pushed the control column forward and the nose dipped. 'I'll line up on the left-hand boat,' he said.

'Thanks!' The technician sat forward eagerly.

'Navigator!' the pilot called. 'Distance to target?'

'Eight miles, boss!'

The plane roared on over a darkening sea.

'Change ships!' the technician ordered and the nose of the aircraft started to swing away.

'Three miles to target,' called the navigator.

Now, only the navigation lights on either ship were visible and in a few more seconds, they too would be left behind.

And then:

'Contact!' A strange, high-pitched electronic whine filled the cockpit.

'That's it!' the technician yelled, his fingers busy with the RDF receiver. 'That's the ship!'

'Navigator! Get a fix!' the pilot called as they roared overhead. He turned and snatched a quick look back but both ships had already disappeared into the darkness.

'Have you got it?' he demanded.

'Affirmative,' the navigator replied.

The technician was almost bouncing up and down in his seat with excitement.

'Fantastic!' he cried. 'Can you send it back right away? It's what they're all waiting for!'

Chapter 52

The atmosphere on board the warship was tense. Tom, Nancy and Sergeant Chung stood at the back of the bridge keeping out of the way. The frigate was at action stations as she raced through the night towards the *Azura*. She was in total darkness and the discreet purple lighting on her bridge could not be seen five metres outside the ship. Only the tumbling wave at her bows marked her passage through the swell.

Inside the frigate, twenty well-armed marines sat patiently waiting for the order to lower their assault boats and board the *Azura*. A helicopter stood silently on the rear deck, its blades bending and dipping in the rush of air. Her pilot was already strapped in, ready for the order to start up.

'His job is to hover above the *Azura*, turn his searchlight on and illuminate the bridge and main deck for the marines' assault,' Sergeant Chung told Tom in a low voice.

The naval captain picked up his handset. 'Ops room! Bridge here. How far to target?' His voice echoed around the bridge.

'Five miles, sir.'

'Bring the speed down to ten knots,' he ordered. 'I don't want some sharp-eyed pirate spotting our bow wave.'

'Roger!' came the reply.

The captain turned in his chair. 'You people all right back there?'

'Yes, sir,' Sergeant Chung assured him.

'Don't worry, Tom,' the captain called. 'We'll soon have your father safe and sound.'

The minutes ticked slowly past. Then, he was issuing more orders.

'Ops room! Bridge. Get the marines up on deck. Stand by to lower boats. And drop the speed to five knots.'

Nancy shivered. 'Tom?' she whispered.

He put his head very close to hers.

'This is for real, isn't it?' she asked.

He swallowed. 'Yes. 'Fraid so.' He remembered the Commissioner's final briefing under the glare of the overhead lights.

'If they've broken down, they'll be on emergency power,' he had told them. 'So we can assume that the *Azura*'s radar will not be working. Which means we can get in close and board her silently. The pirates won't be expecting any such attack.'

It had sounded very reassuring back at police headquarters. But out here, on the ocean, minutes away from life or death, Tom was not so sure. What happened if something did go wrong? Especially if the pirates saw the marines approaching? What if they began to kill the hostages? His father would be the first they'd drag out.

'Ops room! Bridge. Stop engines. Lower boats. Marines to assault stations. Helicopter to take off in twelve minutes' time!'

They heard the orders being acknowledged. Sergeant Chung put a hand on Tom's shoulder and gave it a quick squeeze. Tom smiled back. There was a lump in his throat.

'Ops room! Bridge. Boats away. Commence assault!'

Tom thought he saw a shadow detach itself from the hull of the warship and a brief surge of wash. Then it was gone.

'Not long now!' the captain called cheerfully.

Chapter 53

Duang leant against the bridge wing and fingered his knife. It was a relief to be out here under the stars. Now that there was no longer any air-conditioning, the bridge was like an oven. But it would be ten times worse down in the engine room where those damn engineers and that Captain Lee man were imprisoned.

Duang smiled at the thought. Serve them right! They had sabotaged the ship. His ship. They had tried to get the better of him. By rights, he should kill the lot of them. Lee for certain. And that chief engineer of his. The two of them were in it together.

He looked out across the sea. The tug should be here in a couple more hours. And it couldn't come soon enough. A thought struck him and he frowned. It might be difficult getting rid of Lee after the tug arrived. The Family wouldn't want the crew of the tug to know what was going on. And especially not hear or see things they weren't supposed to. And what happened if something went wrong? Or Lee somehow got on board the tug itself? He was a tricky customer.

Thoughtfully, he lit a cigarette. Should he kill Lee now? There was always the chance of the body hanging around in the water for the next couple of hours or so. He couldn't risk someone on the tug seeing it. Unless, of course, the sharks found it first, and there were a lot of them about. He had seen several fins earlier that evening.

What was that noise? He put his head on one side and listened. It sounded like an engine. Was it the tug? He looked around but could not see any approaching lights. Then a pirate playing an old transistor radio crossed the main deck below. Duang cursed and yelled at the man to turn it off.

There was something moving out there! A dark shadow against the night. He was sure of it. And the sound was like a wasp buzzing in another room. Pirates! he thought. And laughed out loud. The next sound shivered the hairs on the back of his neck. A helicopter had started up! Helicopters meant the police or, worse still, the military.

For a split second, he hesitated. His crew were

scattered all over the ship. There was no time to warn them. And if it was the military, there was no point. He remembered the money in the safe and rushed back inside the bridge. The key turned easily. Duang began to stuff bundles of notes into his pockets then down the front of his shirt. The helicopter was hovering overhead!

He was back outside and running aft when the entire deck was flooded with brilliant light. He tensed, waiting for the bullets to hit him. He saw the familiar shape of a life-raft stowed by the stern. He dashed towards it, untied the lashings and heaved it overboard. He swung his legs over the rail and let go.

He slid down the side of the *Azura*, his back scraping against the hull. Too late, he remembered the propeller waiting below and screamed as his knee smashed against a giant blade. The next moment, the sea closed over his head and he was struggling to get back to the surface. He came up fighting for air. In front of him, the life-raft was inflating and swinging in the current. In another minute, it would be out of reach.

With his useless leg dragging behind him, Duang used every last ounce of strength to reach it. By the time he got there, he was exhausted and could only hang on to the safety ropes looped along its side.

He twisted his head and looked back into the glare. The ship was already some distance away. He saw soldiers clambering up the side of the *Azura* and running along the deck. He could hear firing and a series of small explosions. Then the wash from an assault boat slapped him in the face and he choked.

A little later, he tried to heave himself into the life-raft. But by now, his leg was a complete dead-weight, dragging him down. Duang sank back into the sea and clung for his life to the side of the raft. Although he did not know it, he was bleeding steadily from his badly torn leg.

Chapter 54

Tom heard the helicopter start up and rushed to get a better view. It rose bellowing into the night, hovered for a moment above the warship and swooped away. Seconds later, it roared past the frigate's bridge. Tom caught a brief glimpse of the pilot against the glow of the instrument panel. Then both were swallowed up in the darkness.

'They'll hear it! They'll hear it coming,' he hissed in sudden panic. Nancy stared at him wide-eyed. What could they do? she thought.

Tom peered through his binoculars, searching for the machine. The next moment, he gave a cry of surprise. The helicopter's searchlight had flicked on and the night was transformed. The *Serota Star* lay motionless directly ahead of them. Tom gasped. She looked like some huge toy. Somewhere on board her, his father was a prisoner. He might be shut in a cabin or keeping watch on the bridge. Tom prayed he was safely locked away. The bridge was the marines' first objective!

'There they go!' the frigate's captain called.

Now Tom could see small black figures running aft towards the bridge. And into a sudden burst of gunfire. Lines of red tracer sped towards them. Bullets ricocheted off the deck and went howling into the night.

'They're making a fight of it!' the captain cried in disbelief. 'That was a grenade!' He snatched up his handset. 'Ops. Bridge! I'm going alongside. Looks like trouble. Full speed!'

Tom felt the deck tremble below his feet. The seconds ticked away, then;

'Shooting at the helicopter, sir!' someone called.

'Gun crews close up!' The captain looked round quickly at Sergeant Chung. 'Never known them do this before!'

A radio crackled and a breathless voice filled the warship's bridge. 'We've got two men hit. One badly. Will need urgent medical help.'

Tom and Nancy stared in horror at each other. Sergeant Chung cleared his throat but said nothing.

'We've secured the bridge,' the voice went on.

'Starting to clear below decks. No sign of the proper ship's crew or—' The voice stopped in mid-sentence. For a moment, they listened to the shouting and muffled gunshots, before the voice continued, 'Looks like there's a fire fight above the engine room!' Then the radio went dead.

Sergeant Chung swallowed hard and leant towards the boy. 'It'll be OK, Tom! These men know what they're doing.'

Tom felt sick. No one had said anything about a 'fire fight'. He stared helplessly at the *Serota Star*. His father was right in the middle of it. Helpless. A hostage of no further value. Someone who knew too much. And that could be his death sentence. Dad! Oh Dad! Look out!

Chapter 55

'For heaven's sake! How much longer are they keeping us down here?' Captain Lee exclaimed. 'This heat is torture.'

The chief engineer rubbed a filthy sleeve across his brow. 'Until the tug arrives. If we're lucky.'

Captain Lee stared at him. 'What do you mean, "if we're lucky"?'

'They might kill us before it gets here. Well? Why not?' he challenged, seeing the other's expression. 'We've only got their word they'll let us go at the other end. Now they've got a tug, they don't need us any more.'

Captain Lee's face crumpled. 'Everyone? You think they'll kill Tom as well?'

The chief shrugged. 'I'm sorry! But he's unnecessary too!'

Captain Lee slumped against the silent propeller shaft. 'You always were a pessimist, Chief!'

'Maybe. But I prefer the word "realist"!'

Captain Lee considered this. 'So where are they all? The pirates, I mean?' he burst out. 'There's only one of them down here.' He indicated the man who sat slouched nearby. He was chewing gum dispiritedly. A rifle lay across his knees.

'Apart from our friend over there,' the chief told him, 'the rest of them will be sleeping up on deck if they've any sense.'

'Where we should be. Not stuck down here in this oven.' Captain Lee broke off. 'Hey! What was that?'

They listened, watching each other's faces with growing alarm.

'It's shooting!' the chief exclaimed. 'Listen! There's a battle going on up there!'

On the catwalk above their heads, an outside door clanged open. A pirate burst through. He had a gun in his hand. Three more followed at his heels. They ran in a cursing, jostling mob towards the metal ladders that led down into the engine room. Their guard scrambled to his feet and yelled at them.

'What the hell's going on!' the chief shouted.

'Get down!' screamed Captain Lee, as uniformed

men flooded on to the catwalk. Marines in camouflage smocks raced in pursuit, their boots thudding on the steel deck. The guard loosed off one shot, hesitated, then fired continuously. The place was full of shouting and confusion and the deafening crack of bullets. Something hard hit the propeller shaft beside the chief and left a gleaming scar. A soldier stumbled and fell awkwardly. His rifle fell butt first on to the engine room floor, ten metres below.

A knife flashed close to Captain Lee's head. He ducked and tried to squirm away. Hands tore at him, catching at his hair, yanking his head back. He lashed out with all his strength but was no match for the pirate.

This is it! he thought as an arm pinioned him by the neck. He was aware of the knife held high over his face. He hurled himself to one side and tried to pull the pirate off balance. Then he was staring directly up at a soldier on the catwalk. The man was hurling something at him. It looked like a cricket ball. A split second later, there was a blinding flash, a terrible bang and he pitched head first down a shaft that stretched away for ever, into total blackness.

Chapter 56

In the pink light of dawn four miles east of the *Azura*, a life-raft bobbed. An offshore current was taking it further out into the South China Sea. Its radar reflector had been damaged when it hit the water. There was no trace of it anywhere on any radar screen.

Duang still hung from the looped lifeline. Although the sea was warm, he was starting to shiver. The coldness in his damaged leg was creeping up into his thigh. The pain was now a constant throb and he was still losing a trickle of blood. He had given up trying to haul himself inside the raft. Each time he had tried, he had failed and only felt weaker. He kept telling himself that it was simply a matter of time before he would be spotted by a passing ship. Just so long as he kept clear of the *Azura* and the navy ship.

He must have drifted off to sleep because he woke in

a panic with his face underwater. He came up, spluttering and coughing seawater. The life-raft was some metres away and he splashed noisily towards it. He was not an imaginative man but the sight of the life-raft drifting away made him fully realize the danger he was in. Catching up with it was one of the happiest moments of his life.

He watched the smoke from the frigate's funnel disappear. By this time too, all he could see of the *Azura* was the top of her funnel. The sea around him seemed empty of shipping. Impatiently, he threshed at the water with his good leg to get more warmth into his body.

The sound of his splashing carried a long way under water and gave the great fish the last piece of information it needed. The twelve-foot-long tiger shark had picked up the faint trace of blood some time ago. It had been casting backwards and forwards over a wide area trying to find the source.

Its acute sense of hearing immediately identified the direction of the sounds. It turned to home in on the clear signal of a creature in distress. Soon, it was gliding just below the surface and picking up the strengthening taste of blood. Its dorsal fin rode high out of the sea, parting the water in a ripple of menace.

Something flickered at the corner of his eye and Duang looked to see what it was. The next instant, he screamed. He tried to heave himself into the raft again. The shark felt his terror. The taste of blood was by now in the front of its mouth. But the size of the raft made it wary. Duang's bulging eyes followed its bulk through the clear blue water as it made a pass only a few feet below him. Then it flicked over and disappeared.

At the bottom of its dive, the shark jackknifed, swung its tail to build momentum and came racing up out of the depths. Duang was hurled six feet into the air. He fell back on top of the raft roaring in terror, his fingers scrabbling for purchase on the hot, dry fabric. He fell into the sea with a loud splash. He tried to swing his legs up parallel to the side of the raft but they wouldn't move. He grabbed at the lifeline with both hands and began to sob.

Chapter 57

'I used to go with my husband on most of the raids,' the Dragon Lady said.

'He was a legend in his own time,' Lin Pao assured her, politely.

The two of them were on the bridge of Duang's boat. The village was an hour behind them but in reality, a lifetime away. The sun was hot and the sea sparkled. The boat was clipping along at twenty knots, its engine running sweetly.

'There're not many like him these days,' he added.

'None! They're all clumsy fishermen. No finesse.'

'Didn't your husband invent the "Dragon's Collar"?'

She chuckled. 'That's what the American newspapers called it. We had to lie low when that story got out. That was about thirty years ago, mind.'

'So what happened?'

'We boarded an American freighter. I think she was carrying rice. Anyway, they gave us a lot of trouble. We put the collar on them all but one man survived. He was picked up in the water and told the press.

'I can still smell it now. Rotten meat. How it stank! He used to tie it round the sailors' necks. The sharks would come from miles. You could watch them.' She took a deep breath. 'Those were the days, Lin Pao.'

He nodded in surprised agreement. He had never known her to be so forthcoming. She was almost approachable. He shot a sideways glance at her. There was no doubt about it. She was enjoying herself.

The Dragon Lady felt the rush of wind on her face. The smell of the sea filled her nostrils. She was a young woman again and her eyes sparkled. She remembered all the many times she had done this, with a crew hungry for action and merchant ships spread out before them, like a flock of plump young pigeons.

'It was easier in my day. We often attacked in broad daylight.'

Lin Pao looked surprised. 'I never knew that.'

She nodded. 'Ships were smaller then and easier to board. Their communications were primitive. Most didn't even carry a full-time radio operator. Those that did just tapped out Morse. There were no satellite telephones. Nothing like that. So the authorities were always hours too late to do anything.'

'It was still very brave of you to board in daylight,' Lin Pao mused. 'Didn't they try and fight?'

She laughed. 'That's where my husband was so clever. Everyone knew about that collar of his. Once you picked out a ship, the crew panicked. They were terrified. They had all heard what we might do.'

'Didn't any of the others come to their aid?'

The Dragon Lady curled her lip. 'They just increased speed and ran for it.' She looked at him and frowned. 'Duang should be there by tomorrow afternoon if that tug business went well. I'm sorry it couldn't have been you, Lin Pao.'

He smiled at the unexpected compliment and bowed his head.

'Always the naval officer, Lin Pao! You'll never change. Here! Let me take the wheel. I'll show you how a pirate's wife can handle a boat like this!'

She took the wheel. Chou put his head out of the cabin and looked around. Seeing her there, he hastily made his way forward. The Dragon Lady opened the throttle wider. Soon the bows began to rise as the boat built up to full speed.

'She eats fuel,' Lin Pao shouted, watching the rev counter climb.

The Dragon Lady waved his objections away. 'Just this once, Lin Pao. Just this once. Let an old woman dream.'

A mile ahead and directly in front of them, a twenty-metre-long container wallowed in the sea. It was painted grey and had been washed off the deck of a ship in the last storm. It was almost waterlogged. As the swell flowed over it, the container disappeared below the surface. Afterwards it reappeared, spilling water along its length. It presented a ninety-centimetre-high, reinforced steel side to the world.

By now, the boat was rocketing across the water, throwing out great sheets of spray. The pirates were all on deck, hanging on and shouting excitedly, as the hull banged and crashed through the tops of the waves.

A hundred metres short of the container, Chou straightened up. He leant sideways, peering ahead at something he thought he had seen. He caught another brief glimpse of the container. The boat lurched and he had to hang on with both hands not to fall overboard. Then he began to shout and frantically wave one hand over his head.

On the bridge, Lin Pao stiffened. He knew Chou

well and trusted him. Something was wrong.

'Stop the engine!' he ordered. 'Bring her round!' He waited a moment. 'Do what I say!' he shouted. He grabbed the wheel. She tried to push his hand away. He shouldered her out of the way.

The container surfaced immediately in front of them. It drained water like some grey reef. A helpless Chou watched it coming up out of the depths towards them. By then they were flashing over it.

There was a shuddering crash. The boat was hurled up into the air at an angle of forty-five degrees. The weight of the engine acted as a giant pivot and the momentum did the rest. For a terrible moment, the boat hung vertically. Then it skidded across the sea on its stern. With a neck-breaking jerk, it flipped upside down and ran another fifty metres, its propeller still racing. It sank quickly in a spreading stain of oil and wreckage.

Chapter 58

Captain Lee woke up gradually. He was aware he was in a bed with a sheet on top of him. It felt crisp and starchy. He could smell food and what he thought was disinfectant. He heard a police siren wailing and knew he couldn't be at sea. He was not in any pain although there was a light ringing sound in his ears. It was not a problem. He could hear people talking nearby. He wondered who they were but was really too tired to care. It was time to go to sleep again.

'You've got visitors!' the nurse announced with a smile.

Captain Lee put down a newspaper as Tom, Nancy and Mrs Lee crowded into the room. He held out his arms in delight and for the next few minutes Tom and his mother took it in turns to hug him.

'This is Nancy!' Tom said breathlessly. 'She helped

me steal the boat and cross the Straits.'

'She's a very brave young woman,' Mrs Lee added with an admiring shake of her head.

'I couldn't wait to get away,' Nancy said shyly as Captain Lee kissed her on the cheek.

'She was a prisoner there for three years,' Tom told him.

'So what kept you?' Captain Lee asked.

'Waiting for Tom,' she replied and they all laughed.

Mrs Lee bent down and picked up her husband's newspaper. '"Voyage of Death",' she read aloud.

'We're in all the papers,' said Tom cheerfully.

Captain Lee nodded. 'And they're right! Poor old Robert.' There was a long silence. Then he sighed. 'Still, no one else got hurt.'

After a moment, Tom said, 'Dad, did you know there's an armed guard down the corridor?'

'No! What's he there for?'

'There're two wounded pirates in one of the rooms. He's guarding them. They're going back to prison this afternoon.'

'I heard the marines were lucky,' Captain Lee said. 'Only three wounded.'

Mrs Lee shook her head. 'That's bad enough.'

'Can you remember much?' Nancy asked shyly.

Captain Lee grimaced. 'It's a bit confused. But I remember the stun grenade. That man saved my life!'

'He's coming to see you this afternoon,' Mrs Lee told him. 'He's a Corporal John.'

'And there'll be lots more TV cameras and photographers!' Tom grinned. 'We've all been invited!'

There was a knock and Sergeant Chung stood in the doorway. Tom gave a whoop when he saw him and Mrs Lee hugged him.

'Just to let you know,' he told Captain Lee, 'your ship is back in Singapore.'

'And the crew?'

'Being checked over in a local hospital. They're fine. A bit shaken but fine.'

'What about the cargo?'

'Intact. It's being transferred to another ship.'

'Any more news of the pirates?' Tom asked.

'Have you found Duang?' Nancy demanded.

Sergeant Chung shook his head. 'No sign of Duang, I'm afraid. But if he's hiding on the ship, we'll find him. The rest of them are safely locked up.' He looked at his watch. 'Here's some good news. The Malaysian navy reached the pirates' base half an hour ago. I'll let you know what happens next. I'm looking forward to meeting your Dragon Lady.'

In an instant, Tom was back in the little village. He could see the house on the hill. And the cook and the cage. The sea snakes swimming under the jetty. He remembered Lin Pao and the fog that had saved them. He shivered.

Nancy played with a strand of hair. 'Will you tell them to look out for Duc To?' she asked Sergeant Chung. 'And make sure he's safe? She turned to Mrs Lee. 'He should have been with us on the *Ular Ular*.'

Mrs Lee looked sympathetic. 'I know. Tom told me.' She smiled at the girl. 'So, what's going to happen to you now, my dear? You're very welcome to come and see us whenever you like.'

'That's very kind of you. Thank you.'

Sergeant Chung coughed. 'Mrs Chung and I are hoping Nancy will be staying with us for a very long time. We have an appointment with our lawyer tomorrow to start the ball rolling.'

'That's wonderful news!' Mrs Lee cried. 'You're going to be so happy together! I know it!'

'You will visit, won't you, Nancy?' Tom insisted.

Nancy grinned. 'Just try and keep me away!'

The bedside telephone rang. Captain Lee picked it up. Then he sat up in bed and made frantic signs for them to keep quiet. 'Yes, sir! We're all fine. And the ship's been safely recovered back here to Singapore . . .'

They waited impatiently until he had finished.

Captain Lee looked flushed. 'That was the big chief himself,' he told them excitedly. 'The chairman of South Asia Shipping in person. Calling to see how we all are and with great news, especially for you, Tom!'

They stared at him. 'Well come on! Tell us!' Mrs Lee urged.

Captain Lee laughed in delight. 'He's made Tom an honorary cadet with a guaranteed place in the Line when he's seventeen. Meantime, he can go to sea whenever he wants and they'll pay him.' He grinned at his son. 'There's also a twenty-thousand-dollar reward for him and a generous present for Nancy for their part in saving the *Serota Star* and her cargo. Oh! And I'm to get a new ship!'

He looked around at the smiling faces. 'Congratulations, everyone! It looks as if everything worked out just fine in the end!'

Postscript

Tom has twice been to sea since his fateful voyage in the *Serota Star*. He is keener than ever on becoming a professional sailor. He has not got much longer to wait.

Mrs Lee is now quite happy for him to do so. She doesn't believe anything quite as bad could ever happen to him again. 'Lightning never strikes twice' seems to be her attitude. She will always be very proud of what he did.

Captain Lee was glad to get back to sea. His new ship is large and modern but he will never forget his time in command of the old *Serota Star*.

Tom and Nancy talk regularly on their mobiles. Nancy was adopted by Sergeant Chung and his wife, and has quickly adapted to both home life and school. She wants to be a civil engineer and her teachers think she has every chance of succeeding. She and Tom take it in turns to visit each other.

Sergeant Chung was promoted for his work on the *Serota Star/Azura* case. Mrs Chung is as indispensable as ever to South Asia Shipping Lines.

Mr Patou is serving a five-year prison sentence and is not a happy man. His factory is under new ownership. His old workforce sent him a giant teddy bear last year and a rude note.

Duang's body was found by a fishing boat twenty-four hours after the shark attack. He was still clinging to a safety rope, his fingers stiff in rigor mortis. The fishermen found a disintegrating mass of paper money in the water around him. They salvaged what they could, then slashed and punctured the side of the life-raft. Their last sight was of it tilting heavily to one side, with a legless human body still hanging on.

Nothing more was seen of the Dragon Lady or Lin Pao. Months later, the remnants of a Chinese naval officer's jacket washed ashore on a rocky beach in Malaysia. It is still there.

No one ever saw Duc To again. He was not in the village when the authorities raided it and no one there knew where he had got to. Poor Duc To! He loved Nancy and was heartbroken when she left. His spirit is still probably looking in the village or on the hill for her.

There are other pirates now who have taken Lin Pao and Duang's places. Every year, there are more attacks on shipping passing through the Malacca Straits. At the time of writing, none of the governments which border the Straits have been able to stop them.

Modern-Day Pirates

Twenty-first-century pirates are alive and flourishing. In those parts of the world where they now operate, they are just as ruthless as their historical counterparts and equally successful.

The Malacca Straits that appear in this book are a prime target for pirates. It has become so dangerous to travel through by sea, that in 2003 Lloyds of London classified it as a war zone. One third of all worldwide pirate attacks occur here.

To better understand the extent and range of modern-day attacks on world shipping, I recommend a visit to the International Maritime Bureau's – Piracy Reporting Centre – website: www.icc-ccg.org

This website provides:
• an interactive world map showing successful and attempted pirate attacks;
• a weekly report on current pirate attacks across the world;
• an immediate piracy threat warning to shipping.

In addition, a wealth of information on the Malacca Straits can be found at: www.en.wikipedia.org/wiki/Piracy_in_the_Strait_of_Malacca